# WHAT TO DO

When there appears to be no hope; when all around you are screaming like lost souls, and every spell you try fails to work; when it appears that chaos and evil will at last triumph over good—then, it is truly time for a vacation.

—from THE TEACHINGS OF EBENEZUM,
Volume XXXV

*Don't miss the first volumes
of THE EBENEZUM TRILOGY
by Craig Shaw Gardner:*

**A MALADY OF MAGICKS
A MULTITUDE OF MONSTERS**

# A NIGHT IN THE NETHERHELLS

**Craig Shaw Gardner**

ACE FANTASY BOOKS
NEW YORK

This book is an Ace Fantasy original edition,
and has never been previously published.

## A NIGHT IN THE NETHERHELLS

An Ace Fantasy Book/published by arrangement with
the author

PRINTING HISTORY
Ace Fantasy edition / June 1987

ISBN: 0-441-02314-2

Ace Fantasy Books are published by The Berkley Publishing Group,
200 Madison Avenue, New York, N.Y. 10016.
PRINTED IN THE UNITED STATES OF AMERICA

# ACKNOWLEDGMENTS

The wizard and I go back a long way. I started writing about Ebenezum "way back" in 1977. (In fact, my first major published story was "A Malady of Magicks" in the October 1978 issue of *Fantastic*.) Now, almost ten years later, the Ebenezum Trilogy is finished and in your hands. I couldn't have done it without the help, encouragement, and general all-around browbeating of a lot of people, including Ted White, Orson Scott Card, Marvin Kaye, Lin Carter and Jim Frenkel, who bought the original short stories; my ever-encouraging agent Merrilee Heifetz; and my editor with the great sense of humor (i.e. she likes my stuff), Ginjer Buchanan—along with the rest of the incredibly helpful editorial staff at Ace/Berkley. Thanks, and a tip of Hubert's top hat, are also due to Mary Aldridge, Michael Barton, Stephanie Bendell, Victoria Bolles, Richard Bowker, Jeffrey A. Carver, Amy Sue Chase, Caryl Fox, Charles L. Grant, Heather Heitkamp, Maggie Ittelson, Spike MacPhee, Jonathan Ostrowsky, Alan Ryan, Charlotte Young and Tina Zannieri, for services above and beyond the call of duty.

And then there's my dedication:

*This one's for Elisabeth
especially without whom . . .*

# ONE

*Contrary to rumor, working side by side with a group of fellow wizards is not the most unpleasant task in which a magician might participate. In fact, I can think of numerous other experiences, such as breaking both arms and legs while being pursued by a ravenous demon, which, under certain conditions, could conceivably be even worse.*

*—from* The Teachings of Ebenezum, *Volume XXII*

Vushta was gone.

We stood on the rocky shore of the Inland Sea and stared at the spot where once the greatest city in all the world had reached its towers to touch the sky. How could an entire city simply vanish? I had looked forward all my short life to visiting Vushta, city of a thousand forbidden delights, where great knowledge and great temptation go hand in hand. How I had longed to see the great University of Wizards, and walk the whole length of the Grand Bazaar, and, just perhaps, skirt a corner of the Pleasure District, where, it is whispered, brave men had yielded to their baser drives and had never been seen again. But no, the university, the bazaar, even, yes, the Pleasure District, were beyond me now. Of all the cities in the world, why was Vushta the one to go?

The boatman had left the seven of us here, on the shore which once led to the city that was the goal of our quest. Each of us had had a reason to come on this perilous journey, to come at last to Vushta, a place where we might realize our hopes and cure our ills. Now we were all silent, staring at the empty sky, waiting, perhaps, for the wind to tell us what to do.

"Doom," intoned Hendrek, the large warrior at my side. His great bronze breastplate, which housed a girth fully as wide as he was tall, glinted blindingly in the midday sun. All shade had gone with the city and the wind brought nothing but choking dust.

Hendrek nervously stroked the bag that held his weapon, the cursed warclub Headbasher, which no man could own, but only rent. His mood, I could tell, fit the rest of our small party. The wizard Ebenezum, once the greatest mage in all the Western Kingdoms, and the leader of our quest, stroked his long, white beard reflectively, the tattered remains of his once tasteful robes flapping in the unnatural breeze. The others in our party watched his grim countenance—the demon Snarks, Hubert the dragon and his beautiful companion, Alea, and Norei, the wondrous young witch—all looked at my master, waiting for a decision, or a sneeze.

But the sorcerer breathed deeply, his malady unaffected. If magic had taken Vushta away, it had gone with the city.

The warrior Hendrek took a deep breath in turn. Once again his great voice reverberated across the wasteland.

"Doom!"

"I beg your pardon?" answered a voice from somewhere.

My master waved us all to silence. I held my breath, anxious to hear other words rise from the dust. But the mysterious voice said no more.

"Hendrek," my master said after a moment. "Repeat your curse."

The warrior did as the wizard instructed.

"Doom!"

"Oh!" called the mysterious speaker. "Doom! You see, I thought you were saying 'dune'! Well, there certainly are a lot of them around now, nothing but sand. You'd hardly believe there was a city here only the other day. Still, I didn't know if I wanted to start a conversation with someone who pointed at piles of sand and said 'dune'! But 'doom'? Well, that's another matter. Doom implies angst. I'll always talk to somebody about angst!''

The demon Snarks muttered darkly from deep within his robes. The stranger's monologue had returned the rest of us to shocked silence.

"There!" Ebenezum pointed. From out of the dust before us a figure emerged, clad all in robes as red as blood.

Hendrek pulled his enchanted weapon from his sack. Ebenezum rapidly retreated and held his nose.

"Doom!" Hendrek repeated.

"Yes, isn't it?" the approaching man replied. "Or at least it was the doom of Vushta. I assume that's what you folks came for, to visit Vushta. It's a pity you weren't informed that it was no longer here. But then again, none of us were informed that it was going. One minute there it was, just over the hill, and the next . . ." The newcomer waved a bony hand.

Ebenezum gestured at Hendrek to rebag his club. The wizard stepped forward as the warrior complied.

"Indeed," Ebenezum said. "Have we not met before?"

The newcomer paused a few paces before us. He was a gaunt man, well on in years, his weathered skin pressed tight against skull and finger bones. His whole body—face, hands, and clothes—was covered by a fine layer of dust, which made him appear more ancient still.

"It is possible." The newcomer nodded. "For have we all not met, if not in this life, then on some other plane, or in some prior existence, or perhaps even in the future? For what is time, but an arbitrary structure we mortals—"

"Yes, of course we have met!" Ebenezum cut the other's rambling short. "Are you not an instructor at the Greater Vushta Academy of Magic and Sorcery?"

"Instructor?" The man frowned. "I am a full professor in the college of wizards!"

"Ah, yes." Ebenezum scratched his mustache in thought. "Pardon my oversight. I had forgotten your eminence."

"Quite all right." The old professor smiled again. "Oversight, unfortunately, is common to us all. Reaching for the stars, we lost sight of what is within our grasp. Did I mention that I might have been able to save Vushta? As you see, even a full professor is capable of occasional error. What matters, though, is how we cope with our shortcomings once we discover—"

"Indeed," Ebenezum said with somewhat more force than usual. "And is your name Snorphosio?"

"Why, yes," the elder replied in surprise. "Although what is truly in a name? Is it but a label we hang upon our souls, or do those few syllables somehow imbue us with their essence, in order that we—"

"Indeed!" Ebenezum cried, clasping his hands together so that they might not accidentally do some damage to the old gentleman "And is not your field of expertise theoretical magic?"

"Why, yes." Snorphosio's smile grew even broader. "I like to look at magic in the broadest possible sense. Just what is magic? How does it differ from real life? Or is magic just real life under another name? Or are we just imagining that magic exists? Or are we imagining that real life—"

"I was a student of yours," Ebenezum cut in this time.

"Really!" Snorphosio was delighted. "Did you take 'Basic Theory' or 'Conjuring the Unconjurable'? Do you remember my famous lecture: 'If a Magician Pulls a Rabbit From a Hat, But There Is No Hat, Is There Then No Rabbit?' Oh, I tell you, I always was one for catchy titles."

"Perhaps," my master remarked, "you can tell us what happened to Vushta."

"Vushta?" The professor coughed. "Oh dear, it's

gone. The entire city, buildings, streets, people, animals, every single one of the forbidden delights, sucked into the earth. I could hear their screams when it happened. Horrible!''

"Indeed." My master fixed the professor with his best interrogatory stare. "How did you manage to escape?''

"Easy enough." Snorphosio's smile returned. "I wasn't there. I was visiting East Vushta. Charming little town." The old man peered at Ebenezum. "Hmm. You're getting on in years. Probably a senior wizard by now? East Vushta hadn't really grown up yet when you were in school, had it? Lovely place. Many people have been building small castles there to get out of the rush of the city. That was always a problem with Vushta, you know. It's not easy living in the middle of a thousand forbidden delights, let me tell you!''

"If you could," Ebenezum suggested, "perhaps go into the details of the city's disappearance?''

The frown reappeared on Snorphosio's face. "I'll tell you what little I know. I was sitting in a tavern at the time, in East Vushta, that is. Of course, what I know about this situation is probably more than most other people know. Degrees of knowledge are always relative, aren't they? It reminds me of the parable about the blind men and the dragon—''

Hubert snorted from where he stood some distance down the beach. "Must we?'' the dragon remarked. "I really detest those old stories. Talk about species stereotyping!''

The professor waved cheerfully at the dragon. "Sorry. Didn't see you there. My eyes, you know, are not as strong . . . Still, I suppose that's no excuse for spreading ancient tales." Snorphosio sighed. "The world has changed so much in my day. Once dragons did nothing but hide in caves and collect maidens. Now"—the old man wheezed with laughter—"can you imagine, I actually saw one of the big lizards try to sing in a vaudeville act?''

"Big lizards?" Hubert rumbled. "Alea, if you would hand me the satchel?"

The dragon's beautiful assistant bounced over to him, her blond curls dazzling in the sun. Hubert rummaged quickly through his case, extracting a top hat with one purple claw. He placed the hat atop his head and snorted a cloud of smoke.

"Does this look familiar?" Hubert remarked dryly.

Snorphosio scratched at his chin in consternation. "Damsel and Dragon?" He cleared his throat and looked about as if he might disappear back into the dust. "Oh dear. Well, perhaps I didn't catch you on one of your best nights. All criticism is subjective, as you know. One man's opinion—"

"Indeed!" Ebenezum broke in again. The wizard had backed off for a moment when Hubert stepped in. Because of the nature of his malady, he had to keep his distance from the dragon. Still, this was an emergency. If the old man got off on enough of a tangent, we'd never find out what happened to Vushta.

"I'm sure you can both discuss the merits of the Vushta stage with more enlightenment once we have discovered what happened to Vushta!" the wizard continued. "Snorphosio, if you would be so kind?"

"Of course!" The professor self-consciously brushed the dust from his all-too-red robes. "I did not mean to offend. Still, those in the performing arts must remember that the audience views them subjectively, and inasmuch—"

"Subjectively!" Hubert roared. "That's the problem with you intellectuals. Great art appeals directly to the emotions! Listen to this! Number seven, damsel!"

Alea began to sing in a high, clear soprano as Hubert beat time with his tail.

"Oh, there might be a thousand forbidden delights, but my favorite delight is you—"

"Enough!" Ebenezum cried as he ran between professor and dragon. "Can't you see—can't you—"

My master, the great wizard Ebenezum, fell to the ground in a sneezing fit.

Snarks had his hood off in an instant. "This is impossible! I've known both humans and demons to be longwinded, but this fellow has the lungs of an elephant! And talk about bad taste in clothes!"

My beloved Norei touched my left shoulder. My heartbeat raced.

"Wuntvor!" she cried in a voice more musical than the Vushta stage might ever produce. "We have to do something!"

"A demon's work is never done." Snarks pushed back his sleeves to reveal thin green arms. "Let's drag the wizard out of there."

As briefly as possible, I pointed out to Snarks why this might not be such a good idea. Some weeks past, in the Western Kingdoms where my master maintained his practice, he had accidentally loosed a particularly fierce demon by the name of Guxx Unfufadoo. My master had managed to send that foul fiend back to the Netherhells from whence he had come, but it had cost the wizard dearly. Now, whenever he encountered anything demonic or magical in nature, he would break out in a fit of uncontrollable sneezing. Thus had his current situation been brought about by his proximity to a dragon. If the wizard's proximity to magic ailed him, it did not make sense to have another magical creature come to his aid.

Snarks rolled his sleeves back down. "A demon's work is never appreciated. 'Twas ever thus. Why do you think they kicked me out of the Netherhells in the first place?"

I knew the answer to that, but my master was sneezing far too much for me to reply. I turned to Hendrek for aid. The large warrior and I dragged Ebenezum to a safe distance.

Both Snorphosio and Hubert looked temporarily abashed at what they had caused to happen to my master. Now, I thought, it was time to get to the bottom of all this. And since my master was indisposed, I would have to act in his stead.

"Indeed," I began. "And just what has happened to Vushta?"

"In a physical, or in a metaphorical, sense?" Snorphosio inquired. "Inexact questions, I am afraid, are one of the pitfalls of modern civilization. How many wars could be avoided if we might only learn—"

"Indeed!" I said, rather more loudly. I feared that, should the professor go on at much greater length, I would not be able to match my master's restraint. I glanced meaningfully at Hendrek. The warrior pulled the doomed club Headbasher from its restraining sack.

"Where did Vushta go?" I asked.

Snorphosio looked at the warclub with some alarm. "Now see here, you wouldn't think of using—"

"Doom!" Hendrek remarked. He let the tip of Headbasher fall to the ground. The earth shook.

"Oh," Snorphosio intoned. "Vushta went down."

"Doom!" Hendrek reiterated. "Down?"

"Yes, down. Beneath the earth." The professor's voice dropped to a whisper. "I fear it has been taken by the Netherhells."

Snarks gave a muted cheer. The rest of our company glared at him.

"Sorry," the demon said, embarrassed. "Old habits."

"Oh, Wuntie!" Alea ran up to me breathlessly. "What a diplomat!"

I smiled somewhat foolishly. Alea was an attractive young woman, and, as a professional vaudeville entertainer from Vushta, much more worldly than myself. And yet, long ago, when I was first apprenticed to Ebenezum, Alea and I had shared an innocent young love. Even now, gazing deep into her blue eyes—

"Wuntvor!" Norei was at my side again. "We must have a plan. What shall we do?"

"Yes, Wuntie!" Alea chimed in. "You've gotten us this far. What next?"

I cleared my throat. The young women pressed on either side of me, both far too close. Norei sometimes had trouble with Alea's pet names for me, or the way Alea would refer to things the two of us had done long ago, or the way Alea occasionally treated me as her own personal property. It didn't matter how often I explained that everything that had happened with Alea occurred before I had even met Norei. Well, almost everything. Could I help it if Alea was an attractive and enthusiastic woman? According to Norei, I certainly could.

Norei pinched the flesh of my upper arm in a manner almost too hard to be playful. But I knew that the events around us here had taken a great toll on the young witch, as surely as I knew that she was my own true love. And, unlike my childish infatuation with Alea, what I felt for Norei was a truly mature love, for in the weeks we had been on our quest I had gained experience, responsibility, and insight.

"Doom!" Hendrek said to the three of us. "What shall we do now?"

I had no idea.

"Indeed," I said, stalling for time.

There was a honking sound behind me. I spun about, my stout oak walking staff ready to be used as a weapon if need be. Ebenezum blew mightily into his robes.

"Indeed," the wizard remarked, looking past our party to the somewhat befuddled Snorphosio. "So, if I heard you correctly, the Netherhells have captured Vushta?"

The aged professor nodded rapidly. "That is my surmise. Of course, I am basing this theory upon incomplete evidence. Perhaps my fears are ungrounded. Perhaps something less dreadful has happened to my city than I suspect, some other rationale may be divined from the evidence at hand. For you see"—Snorphosio

paused, his voice dropping to a conspiratorial whisper—
"there is one final event that has not yet occurred, one
last bit of evidence that, were it to be untrue, would
show me for the pessimist that I am. Without this last
event, there is still hope. Perhaps Vushta can still be
saved. Perhaps all of the city's inhabitants will not be
cursed to eternal, unspeakable damnation, the true extent of which is probably beyond human imagining. If
this final catastrophe does not occur, we can still hold
onto a thin ray of hope that perhaps the great city, with
all its learning, its diverse people, its thousand forbidden delights, might yet be rescued. But, should this
event occur . . ." Snorphosio's voice dropped away, as
if the final consequences might be too horrible to even
say aloud.

The silence that followed was shattered by a great
rumble beneath our feet. We had been through Nether-
hells-inspired earthquakes before. I looked for something to hold onto, but there was nothing around us but
piles of sand.

The quake ended before I could even lose my footing.
As I turned to the others, another loud noise erupted
from beyond the dunes, a great, belching roar, as if the
earth itself had swallowed something and found that it
disagreed with its digestion.

Snorphosio had fallen to the dirt. Although the quake
had passed, he was still trembling violently.

"That was the event I was waiting for," the old man
managed after a moment.

"Doom," Hendrek replied.

Snorphosio pushed his hands against the sand to stop
his spasms. He nodded at last.

"All is lost. Vushta is gone forever."

# TWO

*Why don't you conjure a legendary city, full of magic spells and mystic beasts, out of thin air?" the uninformed client asks. "Well, where would you put it?" the wise wizard replies. "Have you seen the price of real estate?*

—*from* Ebenezum the Wizard's Handy Guide to Better Wizard/Client Relationships, *fourth edition*

Vushta was gone forever.

"Indeed," my master said to the cowering Snorphosio. "Are we then the only wizards left in all of Vushta?"

"In all of Vushta, yes, we are the only wizards that remain." The old professor regained his feet somewhat unsteadily. He dusted at his sleeves half-heartedly. "Of course, there are also wizards in East Vushta, some two hills over, but whether East Vushta is part of the greater metropolis has always been open to debate. At the moment, I would imagine that East Vushta is quite separate from the rest of the city." He paused to stare off into the dust. "Yes. Quite separate indeed."

Ebenezum nodded and scratched beneath his wizard's cap. "Wuntvor, shoulder your pack. We all need a place to spend the night. I think East Vushta shall do nicely."

I did as my master bade. The pack, which had once bulged with a large number of sorcerous tomes and arcane paraphernalia, was now much lighter due to the loss of almost the entire contents when I was carried off by a large, mythological bird in one of our more recent adventures. Ebenezum had hoped to replace what he had lost once we reached the fabled centers of learning in Vushta. But that, along with most of the rest of our plans, now seemed futile.

I looked to my master, once the greatest mage in all the Western Kingdoms, as he led our party in a march across the sand. Even though his clothes were torn, his beard matted, his skin burned red by the sun, still he looked every inch the master magician. The casual observer would never have guessed the sorcerer suffered from a malady so great that he must shun all magic; indeed, that the malady affected him to such an extent that he had embarked on a long and arduous journey to seek a cure, even if he had to travel to far, fabled Vushta before he found the knowledge he sought.

And now that there was no more far, fabled Vushta? You would never know it in the way he strode across the dunes, trailed by Snorphosio, who continued to discuss various fine points of sorcery as if some of the others in our party could understand him. Hendrek came next, ever wary, his hand constantly on the sack that carried his enchanted club, a weapon that saw him forever plagued by demons demanding rental payments. He had sought Vushta as well, to free him from Headbasher's dire curse.

All of us had had similar hopes and plans embodied in Vushta. But there had been a further bond holding us together, for, as we won our way closer to Vushta, we discovered an insidious plot on the part of the Netherhells. No longer were these demons satisfied with ruling the world below the earth. No, now they plotted to conquer the surface world as well and subject us all to their fiendish tyranny. Our only hope to stop them was to reach Vushta and alert the Greater Vushta Academy of Magic and Sorcery of the danger. Only with the massed might of the greatest wizards in all the world could we hope to defeat the Netherhells.

A chill ran through my sun-drenched frame. Until now, I had not realized the true enormity of our catastrophe. Vushta was no more. Was there no hope? Had the Netherhells won?

Then we climbed to the top of the second hill and I saw the most magnificent city in the world.

"East Vushta," Snorphosio remarked. "I never realized how small it was until Vushta disappeared."

Small? I might call the vista before us many things, but "small" was not among them. The city seemed to take up the whole valley. Graceful towers of a dozen different colors rose a full three stories above the earth. Furthermore, these great structures were interspersed among literally hundreds of smaller dwellings. There might be a thousand people living here, maybe more. It was enough to take your breath away.

Still, I felt a pang of loss through my sense of wonder. If this vast expanse was only East Vushta, what had the greater city looked like? I felt a prickling sensation at the back of my neck, as if I were being tickled by the ghost of the last, lingering forbidden delight. I was so close! Now, perhaps, Vushta was gone forever!

So intent was I on the sight before me that I did not watch my feet. It was perfectly natural, then, that I should bump into Hendrek's massive bulk, the same bulk that prevented both of us from losing our balance and tumbling down the hill.

"Doom," Hendrek remarked dourly, not noticeably fazed by my abrupt arrival. "Now I will never be free of my cursed warclub."

Snarks walked up and removed his hood. "Don't fret there, Hendy. My demon-trained senses tell me we have not yet found out all we need to know about Vushta's disappearance."

Hope suddenly returned to my despairing frame. I turned to Snarks. "You have discerned some clue as to the Netherhells' plans?"

The demon shook his bright green head. "I just know the way the folks down below work." He pointed forward to Snorphosio. "My theory is that the Netherhells rejected this guy on purpose. Why else would they steal the city only when he was out of town?"

I nodded slowly, not absolutely convinced. Still,

Snarks's surmise did have a certain fiendish logic behind it. Snarks was certainly familiar with the ways of the Netherhells. After all, he had been raised there, though he was different from other demons. Snarks's mother had been badly frightened by demon politicians shortly before he was born. The traumatic experience caused Snarks to develop an overwhelming need to tell the truth, something that can be quite crippling when you're a professional demon. Eventually, it led to Snarks's banishment from the Netherhells, a move which, after hearing some of the demon's choicer remarks, even I could sympathize with.

"Excellent!" my master's voice cried from far up the path we had walked since coming to the valley. He pounded Snorphosio heartily upon the back. Snorphosio almost fell down the hill.

"Wuntvor!" the wizard called to me. "Hurry the others! We must enter East Vushta with all haste! There is still hope!"

I knew my master would think of something! We had come too far on our journey, overcome too many perils. A simple vanished city was not enough to stop someone of Ebenezum's skill and resourcefulness. I ran down the hill to join the mage. So the Netherhells had swallowed Vushta! We would reach down and pull it back to its rightful place, out there amidst the sand.

"Do you have a plan, master?" I cried breathlessly as I slid on a patch of loose earth, tumbling past both wizard and professor.

"Indeed," Ebenezum replied as he walked down to the point where I once again picked up myself and my pack. "As you heard, Wunt, the Greater Vushta Academy of Magic and Sorcery has gone with the rest of the city. The demons apparently wished to imprison all the great mages of this sprawling metropolis, probably to counter any resistance to their fiendish plans for dominance of the surface world. Fortunately for us, demons tend to be very shortsighted. It probably has something to do with living your whole life underground."

"Demonic thought processes?" Snorphosio con-
tributed as my master paused to take a breath. "Do
demons really think? It's a thorny issue. Did you know
their brains are generally green in color? This whole
Netherhells thing may not be their fault, after all. How
would we think with a green—"

"Indeed!" Ebenezum broke in. "Snorphosio was
good enough to inform me as to a point on which I had
been ignorant. While the demons have taken the Greater
Vushta Academy of Magic and Sorcery to no one knows
where, they have completely ignored East Vushta. And,
by doing so, they have completely ignored the Greater
Vushta Academy of Magic and Sorcery Extension Program at East Vushta!"

"Extension program?" I replied, quite confused by
my master's rush of words.

"Why, yes," Snorphosio beamed. "We teach courses
there mostly at night, for part-time wizards. Still, we
pride ourselves on maintaining the same strict standards
for graduating mages that we observe at the day school.
Of course, our facilities are somewhat limited at the
East Vushta location—"

"That may be," Ebenezum broke in, "but there are
facilities! And there are wizards, both instructors and
students, who have come far enough along with their
studies. I tell you, Wunt, it might be possible to save
Vushta after all!"

"Might it?" Snorphosio mused. "Well, I suppose
anything might be possible. That's a problem with
theory, you know—the possibilities are endless. Still,
when you deal with the fine line between possibility and
probability—"

"Indeed!" my master cried. "Lead us to the extension program!"

Snorphosio cheerfully walked to the head of our
party, remarking at some length on the responsibilities
of leadership, and the nature of responsibility, and the
responsibility we all have to nature, and how leadership
within nature makes animals responsible. As he began a

discourse on whether or not animals were responsible to nature within their leadership capacity, we came to a building even more imposing than any we had already seen.

East Vushta was far different from any city I had ever visited. In fact, I realized it was the first group of buildings I had walked through that could truly be called "a city." House followed house, each one made of some colorful stone or preheated brick. There was none of the mud or straw so prevalent in the Western Kingdoms, and none of the one-room hovels that I had lived in most of my life. Dwellings here were built to sprawl and impress. I gazed about me in fascination as we walked to the center of the city. It was almost enough to make Snorphosio's monologue sound interesting.

And now we had come to a large bright red structure, the same color as the old professor's robes.

Snorphosio turned to the rest of our group.

"Gentlemen!" he began. "Um, gentlemen and ladies —um—that is, gentlemen and ladies and assorted non-humans! Welcome to the Greater Vushta Academy of Magic and Sorcery. Or at least the East Vushta division of the Greater Vushta Academy—no, come to think of it, this is now the entire Greater Vushta—"

"Well?" my master interrupted. "Are you going to invite us in?"

"Why, certainly," Snorphosio replied. "Actually, there isn't all that much to see. Well, the dragon may have to wait outside. Low ceilings, you know. But he can follow our progress if he cares to look through the upper-story windows—"

"Indeed," Ebenezum remarked, knocking on the structure's great oak door.

There was no immediate answer, so Ebenezum knocked again. This time he was rewarded by a great deal of creaking and banging from somewhere within.

A small window opened in the middle of the door.

"Go away!" cried a heavily mustached face. The window shutter slammed shut.

"Hmmm." My master tugged at his beard. "Snor-phosio. If you would be so kind?" He indicated the door.

"Certainly." Snorphosio knocked in turn. There was no answer.

My master stepped away from the door. "Hendrek," he called to the large warrior by my side. "I believe this is a job for you."

"Doom," Hendrek murmured as he loosed Head-basher from its sack. He bumped it lightly against the door three times. The door shook. And the small window opened again.

"We don't want any!" the face screamed.

"Doom!" Hendrek replied as he brandished his club.

"Oh," the face remarked. "Well, then again, per-haps we do."

There was a great deal more banging from within. Then the door swung open. The man inside cowered in a corner.

"Spare me!" he cried. "For some reason, they left me in charge. And I'm not even a wizard! They're cow-ards, every sorcerous one of them! I'll be good, I prom-ise. Demonkind forever!"

"Indeed," Ebenezum said, stepping within. "You say that all the wizards have left?"

"Yes!" the other man cried. "And a good thing, too, for what is the pitiful might of wizards compared to the overwhelming strength of demons like . . ." The man's voice faded as he peered at Ebenezum through the gloom. "Wait a second! You're not demons!"

"Well." Ebenezum stroked his mustache. "At least some of us are not."

"Why do you let me go on and on, making a fool of myself? Some people! It's no wonder they left me in charge here, for they knew of my keen wit and my abil-ity to make instant decisions."

The fellow peered more closely at my master's soiled robes. He paused to clear his throat. "Don't get me wrong! Wizards are truly wonderful people. I've worked side by side with them all my life. I respect them even more since they left me in charge. They obviously realize that I'm the only one with the foresight to deal with a situation like this."

"Indeed," Ebenezum replied. "And could you tell me where the other wizards have gone?"

"Gone?" He made an all-encompassing wave with his hands. "Why, home, of course. As I would have done, had not my home been swallowed by the Nether-hells!" The mustached man shivered.

"I see. And do you have a list of their whereabouts?"

"Why, certainly. You are a wizard yourself, aren't you, sir? I pride myself on always being able to spot a wizard. Of course, with your proud bearing and mag-nificent speaking voice, you were all too easy to spot." The mustached man reached within his tunic. "Here. This parchment should give you everything you need. I would stay and chat with you further, but, now that you have come to take possession of the college, I have im-portant business elsewhere. Should you desire any more, don't hesitate to ask next time you see me. Klothus is the name, service is my game."

Klothus nodded, smiled, and walked rapidly toward the door.

Snarks removed his hood to look around. "So this is what a wizards' college looks like. Well, I certainly hope the fellows who built this place know more about magic than they do about decorating."

Klothus gave a small cry when he spotted Snarks's shiny green head, complete with horns.

"Oh, no!" he gasped. "Why, you are demons after all! And here you have, by trickery, gained information about the remaining wizards' whereabouts! Well, I never would have given it to you voluntarily, let me tell you!" Klothus looked around surreptitiously. "Now that it's out, though, it's probably just as well you have it. You'll get the mess over with right away, won't you? I'm sorry I don't have any other worthwhile information. No information at all. So I guess I'll just be running along, and let you demons take over. I tell you, in a way I'm really looking forward to a change in government. The way the wizards ran this city was laughable." But Klothus was not laughing as he shuffled through the doorway.

"I don't think you should leave just yet," said a voice from on high.

Klothus looked up at Hubert. "They've enlisted dragons, too? I had no idea this thing was so large. I admire your planning. I really do. But I must be off—oh—someplace else. Anyplace else . . ." Klothus's voice died in his throat as he watched thick smoke trickle from Hubert's nostrils.

"I think the most important place is right here," the dragon rumbled.

"You may be right," Klothus remarked, backing into the college. "I'm sure whatever you have to say is quite correct." He turned to the rest of us. "This fellow doesn't breathe fire indoors, does he?"

"Indeed!" Ebenezum, carefully keeping his distance from Snarks and Hubert, called from across the room. "However, since you are happy to cooperate with us, I'm sure the dragon's fire will not be necessary."

"So glad to hear that," Klothus responded. "And how may I serve you?"

"As you have discerned," Ebenezum replied, "most of us are new to the city. Therefore, a list of the remaining wizards' whereabouts does us little good without either a map or someone with a good knowledge of the surroundings. We shall need you to go and personally summon the wizards."

"Oh, is that all?" Klothus smiled craftily. "I shall go right away. If you gentle demons will excuse me."

"Doom!" the large warrior grumbled. "We are not—"

"Wait!" Ebenezum cried. "To lighten your burden of responsibility, Hendrek will accompany you."

Klothus's smile vanished. "Why, of course, show someone else the city while I'm at it. Always glad to oblige!"

"Hubert!" my master called to the dragon. "While they are about their business, I think you would do well to circle East Vushta for signs of further demonic activity. Simply because the Netherhells have spared this location so far does not mean that they will continue to do so."

Hubert tipped his hat to the wizard, then handed it to Alea. He turned and launched himself aloft.

Alea waved at the retreating dragon. "Look at that, Wuntie! What dramatic style!"

"Indeed," Ebenezum continued. "And while the rest of you are busy on your various errands, Snorphosio and I will quickly search this place to see what magical materials are still at hand. Go now, Klothus! Tell the wizards to meet us here within the hour."

"Snorphosio?" Klothus exclaimed. "I did not realize Snorphosio was among your number. You could not possibly be in league with demons! Snorphosio is not the type. How do you expect me to draw the proper conclusions if you do not give me all the information?"

"Doom," Hendrek remarked as he approached the gray-clad Klothus. The other man turned and hurried through the door.

"Wuntvor?" Norei was at my side. I felt her hand brush against my hip. It was good, I thought, to have my young witch near in this time of trial.

"Oh, Wuntie!" Alea was at my other side. Her blond hair shone even in the filtered sunlight here in the hall. The room had become uncomfortably warm for so late in the year.

"I shall need all of you as well," the wizard called. "We must search as much of the college as we can before I meet with the other wizards. Wuntvor will take the left corridor, Norei the right, Alea will search the grounds, Snarks the guardhouse, and Snorphosio will see what implements are left in the basement vaults."

"How did you know?" Snorphosio asked. "I must say, you are very perceptive for a younger wizard. I am quite astounded that you discerned that even a college this humble would have an underground vault. Did you see some secret panel, or perhaps some mud of a different color, that led you to suspect some underground—"

"Indeed," Ebenezum interrupted with a wave of his hand. "There are always basement vaults. It is how wizards think. Now go, and report back to me with whatever you find."

"Wizards' thought processes," Snorphosio mused as he walked toward a flight of stairs that led downwards at the rear of the hall. "Now that is grounds for conjecture. How does magic affect thought? How does thought affect magic? How does thinking about magic affect magical thought? How does magical thought affect . . ." His voice was lost as he descended the stairs.

"Indeed," Ebenezum remarked dourly. "Hurry with your search, Wuntvor. I may need you to fetch the professor from down below."

There was one thing I had to know before I left.

"Do you have a plan?" I asked.

Ebenezum pulled reflectively at his beard. "I will by the time the other wizards arrive. The Netherhells have already done their worst. In an hour, Wuntvor, we begin the counterattack!"

# THREE

*The professional wizard, it is said, should always watch his hands. Actually, the truly professional wizard should watch a great many other things as well, including the reactions of his audience, the door or window that constitutes the nearest exit, and, perhaps most important, the constantly fluctuating interest rates on his retirement account in the First Bank of Vushta.*

—*from* The Teachings of Ebenezum,
Volume VI

I walked quickly through the wizards' college, passing from the entranceway into a grand hall high enough to accommodate even Hubert. The whole place was made of stone. Huge blocks had been piled atop one another to make vaulting hallways and even larger rooms. As I walked, I wondered if this whole place might have been built by magic; that perhaps some sorcerer as great as Ebenezum had waved his hands over a patch of ground, and the stones before him had rearranged themselves into this magnificent structure.

It certainly seemed possible. No matter how this place had come to be, it gave one pause for thought. This college of wizards was a place of magic, and within its walls, *all* things were possible. What wonders had been conjured in this great room through which I now passed? Perhaps, on this pink-and-white marble dais before me, a mage produced strange flowers and stranger birds, never before seen by man. Perhaps the audience in this amphitheater had been shown visions of civilizations at the bottom of the sea, or looked above the clouds at cities made all of silk and glass. Or perhaps the scholars at the long table by the door had contented themselves with visits from demons and demigods so they might chat over tea about the meaning of all existence.

I walked from the great hall into a smaller room, a library of some sort, filled with perhaps a thousand books, twice as many tomes as even my master had possessed. My heart raced. Surely we could find something here that might help us to save Vushta!

My eyes eagerly scanned the shelves. There had to be something! Surprisingly, the first book I saw I had used before: *How to Speak Dragon*. My hopes rose. While not perhaps relevant to our current predicament, it certainly was a standard tome for communication between species. I eagerly turned to the next volume on the shelf. It was also *How to Speak Dragon*, as was the one after that. I frowned. Perhaps there was somewhat less variety here than I had first imagined. The same book lined the entire shelf. In all, I counted twenty-six copies.

Still, that left over nine hundred other tomes that might be helpful. I searched about at random through the other books. *Sixty-three Easy Herbal Remedies for Tired Feet* didn't seem to be of any immediate use either, but at least the library carried only four copies of that volume.

I concentrated my search on the lower shelves. Here now were things of more interest: some dozens of copies of *Lives of the Great Magicians, Volume VI: The Clerics*. Any work about magicians should contain some useful spells. I eagerly pulled the book from the shelves. Other volumes were listed on the cover: *The Innovators, The Daredevils, The Pragmatic Geniuses, The Demonologists, The Champions*. This was more like it!

I opened the book at random and quickly read the chapter heading: "Duckwort, the All-Purpose Herb."

All-purpose? Perhaps there was some spell herein for vanquishing demons or retrieving lost cities. How proud Ebenezum would be when I brought him the solution to his problems!

My hopes died as I scanned the pages. The author

went on about how early magicians evolved the proper notation for the storage of duckwort in all its forms, from Highland Golden Duckwort to Eastern Spotted Duckwort, with a special section on how to dry duckwort leaves, duckwort flowers, and duckwort stems. By the time, some twenty-six pages later, I had gotten to the next chapter, "Eye of Newt, the Wizard's Friend," I feared that this book, though certainly thorough, could contribute nothing of any value to our current problem. Still, some other book in the series, say *The Demonologists,* or even *The Champions*, would probably go into exactly the detail we needed.

I ran my finger down the row of identical volumes, for that was what I found—some forty-one copies of *The Clerics* in all. What kind of a library was this, anyway?

I had spent far too long in this small room. I was but a magician's apprentice. Full-fledged mages could probably enter this room and within seconds find the very information they required. I would tell Ebenezum about this place, but for now it was more important that I continue my search. The solution to all our problems might wait just beyond the next door, or beyond the door after that. I had to explore the rest of this wing, and quickly!

The next room was even smaller than the library. It was filled with four long benches, all of which faced another dais, although this one was smaller than the one in the great hall, and fashioned of wood rather than marble. But what interested me most was a chart on the wall, labeled "Simple Magic Production." Here, at last, was something I might be able to use!

The chart showed three objects surrounded by a great deal of script. On closer examination, I realized the pictures were three different styles of hats currently favored by wizards. I assumed this was some sort of hat magic. Ebenezum had never shown me any sorcery of this type, but then my master had had little occasion to show me much of any kind of magic before his afflic-

tion overcame him. Perhaps this chart might be of some
value.

My foot hit something as I walked over to the dia-
grams. It was a hat, probably used for practical demon-
strations. I looked back at the chart. How easy was this
magic to do? Maybe I could return to the others with
something far more practical than books.

The scriptwork around the pictures seemed to be a
series of instructions for the production of flowers,
scarves, and certain small animals. Again, there didn't
seem to be anything of value here to our immediate
problem. But, as long as I had the hat in my hand, what
harm would it do to give the spells a try?

I held the hat, a traditional magician's skullcap,
about a foot away from my chest and made the four
mystic passes called for in the directions. From a quick
reading of the chart, scarves seemed to be the easiest
thing to produce. I said the three words clearly and
reached within the cap.

My fingers grasped something soft. I pulled forth a
scarf of midnight blue!

Excitement almost overwhelmed me. Although I was
a full-fledged magician's apprentice, circumstances had
prevented me from practicing all but the most rudimen-
tary of spells. In addition, due somewhat to haste and
inexperience, many of my earliest conjurations had not
been as successful as I might have hoped. Ah, but this
cap spell was different; the ideal learning tool for the
young magician! I repeated the mystic passes and the
three words. This time I pulled forth a pair of scarves,
one the color of spring leaves, the other the shade of the
sky at dawn. Oh, if only I had had equipment like this in
the Western Kingdoms, by now I might be a full-fledged
wizard!

I turned back to the chart, eager to discern what other
secrets the text might reveal.

It was even simpler than I had imagined. According
to the remainder of the scrollwork, you could simplify

the magic even further, so that each of the three basic conjures could be produced with but a single word. The scroll suggested you start with simple words, such as "yes," "no," and "perhaps," assigning one to scarves, one to flowers, and the third to small animals. I did the necessary secondary conjurations. Wouldn't my master be proud of me when he saw how easily I had acquired a new skill!

"Yes!" I cried with a brief wave of my hand. I reached into the cap and brought forth four scarves tied end to end, red to blue to green to gold.

I laughed and flung the scarves about my neck. "No!" I cried and reached into the cap to pull forth a bunch of daisies.

"Wuntvor?" a soft voice called.

I looked up to see the beautiful Alea watching me through a window.

"Alea!" I cried. She smiled her brilliant smile. Her hair, as always, shone magnificently in the sun. I was holding flowers in my hand. What could be more natural after this than I should give her a gift? True, now that I had Norei, Alea and I were a thing of the past. But it was a fondly remembered past, and Alea's eyes were the blue of summer skies.

"Wuntie?" Alea replied.

"Here," I said, offering the daisies. "It's a gift for you."

"Oh, Wuntie!" Alea squealed. "I'll be right in!"

Right in? I began to object, but thought better of it. How could she have known that I was simply going to hand the flowers to her through the window and then get on with my work? Oh well. I supposed it was a little more romantic this way, and I really owed it to Alea, for what we had once meant to each other. It would only take me a minute to hand her the flowers before continuing my search.

She entered through the far door of the room. She had been running and her chest heaved with the exertion. I marveled at how lovely she looked, even when she was winded.

"Are those flowers for me?" she managed after a moment.

"Yes!" I replied, holding the daisies out to her with my free hand. "I thought it would be nice to give you a little gift, for all that we once meant to each other."

"How sweet!" she exclaimed, taking the bouquet. A beatific smile spread across her face as she smelled the flowers. I noticed that the daisies went quite nicely with her hair.

The hat in my hand suddenly felt heavier. Puzzled, I reached inside and pulled out a large string of scarves.

Alea clapped her hands. "Oh, how clever! Can you do that again?"

"No," I frowned. The number of scarves seemed to be multiplying with every repetition of the key word. "I had better not. I don't want this place to become overrun with scarves."

The hat was heavy in my hand once again. I tipped it over. A much larger bunch of daisies scattered to the floor.

"Oh, how pretty! Are these for me as well?"

I stared at these newly produced flowers with some distress. What had I said to conjure these?

"Wuntie?" Alea prompted.

"Are the flowers for you?" I repeated. "They may as well be, now that they are here."

"Wuntie!" Alea pouted. "That's no way to give a present!"

She was right. Just because the magic had gotten a little out of hand was no reason to be rude. I stammered an apology.

"Don't worry," Alea replied as she picked daisies from the floor. "I know you've been under a lot of pressure lately, what with the disappearance of Vushta and everything." She smiled impishly. "I know of a good way to distract you!"

"Alea?" I said in alarm. I was somewhat disconcerted by her rapid approach.

Her face was incredibly close to mine. Her lips were closer still.

"Anyone"—she was speaking in a whisper both slow and deep—"anyone who gives a woman so many flowers deserves a reward."

And then she kissed me.

"No!" I cried. Didn't Alea know I was promised to Norei? An exchange of gifts was one thing, but kissing . . .

I paused in my thoughts. I had forgotten how well Alea could kiss.

The hat in my hand felt heavier than ever. I tipped it over. An enormous number of flowers fell out.

"Oh, Wuntie!" Alea said with delight. "If that's the reaction I'm going to get, I'll kiss you all day!"

"N—" I began, then thought better of it. I realized now that if I said "no" the hat I held would produce flowers and if I said "yes" it would produce scarves. With the help of the nearby chart, I had made a simple conjuration far too simple. I wondered how I might reverse the process.

Alea used my hesitation to kiss me again.

After a moment, I managed to break free. I shook my head in an attempt to clear it and regain my breath.

"Perhaps," I began, "this could best be saved until another time."

Alea's face was still far too close to mine.

"If you think so, Wuntie," she breathed.

Suddenly, the hat in my hand became so heavy that I almost lost my grip upon it.

"Eep, eep!" said the hat.

"Oh!" Alea cried. "Do you have a bunny rabbit now?"

Bunny rabbit? I had said "perhaps!" I had forgotten about the small animal part of the spell.

"Eep, eep!" the hat repeated. Two dark eyes blinked at me from the cap's dim interior. A long, reddish-brown snout popped out of the cap.

"That's no bunny rabbit!" Alea wrinkled her nose in disgust.

"No," I agreed. "Actually, it looks more like a ferret."

"A ferret?" Alea watched the small, reddish-brown creature as the small, reddish-brown creature watched Alea.

"My father used to keep them," I replied. "The farm where I grew up had moles."

"A ferret?" Alea repeated. She backed away, all thoughts of romance fled.

"Eep, eep!"

The ferret scrambled out of the cap, which was now filled with flowers.

"Wuntvor?" Alea asked uneasily. "Don't you think it's time you stopped making things appear in the hat?"

"Yes, I do!" I agreed, shaking the flowers free. "I just have to figure out how to do it."

Scarves began to boil out of the hat at an alarming rate.

"No!" I cried without thinking, and watched flowers displace the scarves. I let the hat drop. The flowers kept coming.

I pushed past Alea to get a better view of the chart.

"Wuntie! What shall we do?"

"I have to read this," I explained. There had to be some way out of this mess. Everything would be fine if I could only stop this hat producing things before anyone else arrived.

"Oh dear! Is there anything I can do?" Alea asked.

"Yes!" I called back. My voice was somewhat louder and more agitated than it should have been. "Help me read this char—" The hat was producing scarves again.

"No!" I jumped for the hat, trying to push the scarves back inside.

The hat began to produce both flowers and scarves simultaneously.

"Oh, Wuntie!"

I jumped back to her side. "Read!" I insisted. And I did the same.

There didn't seem to be any notation about stopping the simple spell. How could the chartmakers be so shortsighted? Didn't they expect people to practice with their merchandise?

"Wuntie! I can't move!"

Alea was right. The scarves and flowers were so deep around our feet that it was getting difficult to walk. I pulled Alea free of a nasty knot of scarves.

"Perhaps," Alea suggested somewhat hysterically, "if you said the spell backwards?"

"Perhaps you're right!" I replied. It was certainly worth a try. "Sey! On! Spahrep!"

"Eep eep! Eep eep!"

A pair of ferrets leaped from the hat. Apparently, out of everything I'd said, only the "perhaps" had worked. But maybe, just maybe, if I said the complete spells in reverse, I might be able to stop this madness.

"Oh, Wuntie!" Alea grabbed me tight.

"No," I cried. "I have to conjure!"

But Alea held me in a death grip. "At least we will be trapped together," she said, her voice tinged with panic. It was touching, at that moment, that she still cared for me.

Alea sighed, calmer now that she was in my arms. "Still, I had hoped to die with a much wealthier man. Sorry, Wuntie!"

I assured her it was all right as I pushed her delicately away. Perhaps I still could reverse the spell and undo the damage before my master wondered where I had gone.

"I beg your pardon!"

"Someone's here!" Alea regrabbed my neck.

"What is the meaning of this?"

I turned around. Norei stood in the doorway.

I smiled weakly. "It's not what you think. Things have gotten a little out of hand!"

"I should say so!" Norei placed her hands on her hips. "Perhaps the two of you would like to be alone!"

"No!" Alea cried, still keeping me in her strangle-hold. "We need your help!"

I tried to explain, as briefly as possible, about the hat, and the spells, and the innocent gift of flowers to Alea.

Norei nodded when I was through. "So you want to clean up this mess before Ebenezum gets wind of it? It's quite true that he might misunderstand, and get angry with your simple experiments. He probably simply wouldn't comprehend your intense need to play with hats with the situation so serious and all." She bit her lip. "Well, I might be able to do it. Give me a minute to think."

I breathed a long sigh of relief. Ebenezum was a truly mighty wizard, but when he became upset, his anger could be more mighty still. Now he would never have to know. Norei was the savior of us all!

And then a great roar filled the room. It took me but a moment to recognize the sound for what it was: a tremendous sneeze.

# FOUR

*Magicians must exercise caution in all things. Each of you has heard the story of the mage who perfected the gold producing spell, only to be crushed by his newfound wealth. Less well known is the story of the sorcerer who turned everyone he didn't like into a toad, until the day he exercised the spell on an entire unfriendly village and was found the next morning hopped to death. Then, of course, there is the extremely unpleasant story of the wizard who doubled as a gentleman farmer, and his perfection of a manure abundance spell. Whether this latter mage is still alive or not is open to debate, for no one has ever had the wherewithal to visit the scene of his accident to find out.*

*—from* The Teachings of Ebenezum,
*Volume XII*

"Master!" I cried. "Back away quickly. There is too much magic here!"

The sneezing retreated.

Alea clutched me harder than ever. I was finding it difficult to breathe.

"Quickly now!" Norei demanded. "How did this spell begin?"

I paused in my attempt to disengage Alea's grip long enough to point at the chart, now half covered by flowers and scarves.

"Oh," Norei ruminated. "This should be easy enough. But for the spell to really work, Wuntvor, you should repeat my words and gestures."

"Alea!" I insisted. "I need my hands free!"

The woman at last backed away, an odd expression on her face.

"I love a man who speaks with force," she whispered.

I had trouble looking into Norei's eyes. The temperature of her gaze seemed slightly below that of a winter gale.

Norei began to speak, her words as cold as her gaze. Still, I repeated those words and the movements of her hands.

The hat stopped producing things.

"Yes," I said experimentally.

Nothing.

"No," I added. "Perhaps."

Still nothing, not even an *eep*. I let out a great gasp of relief.

Norei was still frowning. "I am glad we were able to cure your problem. I hope you have more success when it comes time for us to rescue Vushta."

"Norei!" I moaned. I wanted to run to her, to try somehow to explain, but Alea was in my way, watching me through half-closed eyelids.

"Oh." Norei turned back to me as she was about to pass out the door. "One more thing. The spell outlined on that chart is almost too simple. Be careful, Wuntvor, to steer clear of the gestures and words you used before, or you might find the hat producing all over again."

All over again? I had a sudden picture of a peaceful afternoon with Norei suddenly overflowing with flowers, scarves, and ferrets.

Norei had disappeared from the room. I grabbed the hat and tore it into little pieces.

"Wuntvor!" It was my master's voice, calling from another room. I hastily tucked the pieces of what was once the magic hat inside my shirt. At the first opportunity, I would toss them down some local well.

"Eep eep! Eep eep! Eep eep!"

Three reddish-brown heads had emerged from the sea of scarves and flowers around my feet.

Alea gave a little cry as she backed away. The three heads nuzzled at my legs.

"Wuntie?" Alea said with wonder. "I never knew ferrets could be so affectionate."

"Eep eep!" said one.

"Eep!" another replied.

"Actually, they're sort of cute this way. They almost act as if you were their mother." Alea giggled. "I suppose in a way you *are* their mother."

The third ferret looked at me with its big brown eyes. "Eep, eep!" it piped happily.

I had to get out of here. My master needed me. Even now, I could not think of ferrets as cute.

"You know," Alea said slowly, that dreamy look back in her eyes, "maybe I should reconsider marrying a wealthy man. Being a good parent can be so important!" She stroked my shoulder meaningfully.

I gave Alea a final smile as I dodged her grasp.

"Watch the ferrets for me, will you?" I called as I leaped free of the scarves and ran from the room, leaving a cry of "Wuntie?" and a chorus of "Eeps!" behind me.

"Wuntvor!" the wizard called again. If anything, he sounded more agitated than before.

"Yes, master?" I replied. If I had to face Ebenezum's wrath, I might as well get it over with. I ran back through the library into the large hall, where my master waited for me with a dozen others.

"So good of you to free yourself," my master said upon my arrival. He smiled coolly in my direction. I tried to smile back. Apparently, Ebenezum did not feel it seemly to show his anger in front of so many others. Somehow, the smile he showed me was almost worse.

"This is my apprentice," the wizard remarked to the others. "Now that he is here, I think we should all take a moment to become acquainted. I am Ebenezum, a wizard of some repute from the Western Kingdoms, here in Vushta as the result of a personal quest. Some of you I already know."

He nodded at Alea as she entered the room at my heels. My master quickly introduced Snarks, Hendrek,

Alea, and Norei, and alluded to Hubert as "that dragon out in the courtyard."

"Two others here I think we all know: Snorphosio, a professor of some repute here at the university; and Klothus . . ." My master hesitated. "Indeed. In my haste, I neglected to ask Klothus just what function he did perform." He nodded at the man in gray. "If you would be so kind?"

Klothus took a deep breath and tilted his head upward, as if he might look down his nose at my master. Since Ebenezum was considerably taller than the man in gray, this gesture was not as successful as it might have been.

"I," Klothus stated, "am the assistant royal costumer for all of Greater Vushta!"

"Indeed?" My master smiled. "An honorable profession, and one that is of great service to all other professions."

Klothus nodded soberly. "I am glad you understand me."

"Indeed." My master tugged at the remnants of his robes. "By the way, do you think you might find the time to get me a new set of these?"

Klothus nodded. " 'Tis the very reason I am here, to refit all the wizards of the extension program with new robes befitting their station."

"Excellent!" Ebenezum clapped his hands together in approval. "Then I should tell you that the robes I always wear—"

Klothus stamped his foot in agitation. "No, no, don't say another word! I know at a glance what you need! It was no accident that Klothus has risen to the top of his profession!"

"Just so." My master scratched absently at his left eyebrow. "Now, if those here whom I have not yet met might do me the honor of introducing themselves?"

The half dozen newcomers each said a few words. Four of them were part-time students, not far along the way with their studies. The fifth was a professor, also dressed in red. However, it was there that his similarity to Snorphosio ceased. His name was Zimplitz. He was stocky where Snorphosio was thin and shouted when the other professor muttered.

"I am in charge of all the practical field magic," he concluded. "You know, directed studies." He pounded the table before him for emphasis. "Places where wizards can get their hands dirty!"

Snorphosio sniffed at the other professor's enthusiasm. "Alas, that most wizards choose to ground themselves in something so common. If more mages were to think on the theory behind their craft, imagine what heights we might have—"

"Yeah, yeah," Zimplitz interrupted. "I know all about your lectures on imaginary rabbits and imaginary hats. Well, let me tell you all something. When we find a hat in Field Magic, we darn well use it!"

I glanced at my feet and quietly wished the talk would move away from hats. It occurred to me that the pieces of one such magic cap were still tucked within my shirt. I really would have to get rid of them at the first convenient opportunity.

"I-Imaginary rabbits?" Snorphosio sputtered. "Imaginary hats? I'll have you know that my students can pull—"

"Indeed!" Ebenezum cried. "And I'm sure both of you are perfectly correct. But there is still one gentleman here yet we have to meet."

The last of the newcomers nodded at my master and smiled uncertainly. The fellow was every bit as tall as me, and probably better muscled. He doffed his hat before he spoke.

"My name is Tomm," he said in a voice barely audible. "And I am but three credits short of my wizard's degree. I would have had it already but that I have to pursue my humble craft to pay my tuition."

"Excellent!" my master said. "And what craft do you pursue?"

Tomm hesitated, looking at the floor much as I had

but a moment before. "You see, good sir," he began, "I have attended wizard school to improve myself, to change my lot in life. I . . ." He paused, as if he might choke on the words. "I am a tinker." He raised his hands to stay any comments from the rest of us. "Some of you may wonder what troubles me so. Surely, you will say, it is an honorable trade. But how many of you, day in and day out, when asked about your occupation, must say 'I tink'?"

Tomm paused and let out a long sigh. His eyes rose to meet my master's gaze. "But I have nearly finished my wizard training. Soon tinking will be a thing of the past. But I have another shame that may be more difficult to live down."

We all stared at the tinker in silence. He swallowed hard and continued to speak in a voice barely above a whisper.

"I might have been able to save Vushta, but I ran away instead."

"Aren't you," Ebenezum replied, "being a bit hard on yourself? The power to make a city the size of Vushta disappear is great indeed. Can you berate yourself for being only one man, facing all the might of demonkind?"

"Yes, I can!" Tomm shouted with surprising force. "I was near the center of it all! I could have stopped it, I know. I was in Vushta mere moments before it disappeared!"

Tomm shuddered. "Let me tell you my story, and you will know my shame."

Quickly, the young wizard-to-be told his story. He had been on his way to his weekly visit with his aged mother when he noticed things were changing. Great black clouds covered the sky to turn it dark as night, brightened suddenly by jets of flame, appearing with blinding suddenness high in the heavens.

"Doom," Hendrek remarked.

Tomm nodded. "I thought so as well. I hurried into the dwelling where my mother had a room on the very top floor, taking the steps two, even three at a time. I prayed nothing was wrong. I knew if anything happened to my mother, I would never forgive myself!''

Tomm paused again to take a ragged breath.

"And?'' Zimplitz prompted. All of us had gathered close to the overwrought tinker.

"I knocked upon the door.'' Tomm's lower lip began to tremble.

"And?'' Alea whispered. The look of concern upon her face seemed to light her blond curls from within.

Tomm's voice was nothing more than a croaking whisper. "And my aged mother answered it.''

I noticed my master pulling his beard with some agitation. "Indeed?'' he said. "Then what was the problem?''

The tinker looked to my master and Ebenezum's authoritative gaze seemed to calm him.

"She told me to be quiet,'' he said in a voice both louder and calmer than before. "She had some sort of pest in her apartment. I noticed then that she was holding her umbrella. A pest, I thought? Surely it was only a mouse or some large insect I could easily catch and remove. My mother's eyesight is not what it once was, so it could not have been something really small. But when I saw the pest she spoke of . . .'' His voice died again.

"And?'' Norei urged, her hands before her as if she might pull the words from his lips. The tinker had gone too far to stop now. Like me, I was sure she wanted to shake the young man until his entire story came spilling out.

"First, I heard the voice,'' Tomm continued, his own voice not so calm and not so loud. "If you could call it a voice. I knew from the first words that the speaker was not human! It sounded like the deep groan of an unoiled gate, crossed with the noise of a giant crushing rocks beneath his feet. And the words this inhuman voice spoke!

" 'Come my demons, now arise,

" 'For Vushta is our greatest prize!' "

"Guxx!" I cried. The tinker had encountered the dreaded rhyming demon!

My master waved me to silence and bade Tomm to continue.

"You know of this fearsome creature?" Tomm said, awestruck. "Well then, perhaps you will understand my weakness. I strode forward as if in a dream to confront whatever inhuman force had invaded my mother's dwelling place. After all, was I not a wizard, only three credits shy of my diploma? Thus it was that I stepped boldly out on the balcony and confronted the largest demon I had ever seen!

"Some of you have already seen Guxx. I do not need to tell you about his bright blue scales, or the size of his teeth and claws. Perhaps, if I had had but a moment to collect myself after our first confrontation, I might have discovered some way to deal with this fearsome apparition before me. But, you see, there was my aged mother . . ."

Tomm's voice once again caught in his throat, but he cleared it and went on before any of us could prompt him further.

" 'Where is that pest?' she shouted. 'I'll show you what happens to things that materialize on my balcony!' And she swung her umbrella high above her head.

"The demon snarled at her:

" 'Begone old woman, do get back,

" 'Or Guxx shall eat you for a snack!'

"Well, what was a son to do?" Tomm sighed. "My mother was always a woman of spirit!"

"Amf?" Snarks cried from deep within his hood. Would this tinker never finish his story?

Tomm shook his head. "I didn't even think of spells, only of protecting my dear old mother, who was busily beating her umbrella against the monster's head. And how did the demon react to my attack?"

Tomm laughed. "The demon took me in one large clawed hand and tossed me from the balcony as he shouted out another rhyme:

" 'No more worry, no more fuss!

" 'Vushta now belongs to us!'

"There was a great crashing roar, and I was sure it was my death. But, a moment later, I found I had landed safely in a pile of sand. And, once I had regained my breath and the dust had cleared, I discovered Vushta had disappeared!"

"Indeed," Ebenezum said when it became apparent that Tomm was done with his tale. "I know far more of Guxx than you can imagine. You should not berate yourself, for you had no chance of success. The foul demon's power grows with every rhyme he makes, and it sounds as if Guxx was in prime rhyming form. Amazingly, even his meter was more or less correct. Against odds like that, even the greatest magicians in Vushta would have little hope."

"Doom," Hendrek added.

"Most interesting," Snorphosio commented. "Guxx is involved, then? That does change our perspective on the seriousness of the situation. As all good theoretical magicians know, Guxx Unfufadoo is the sort of demon that must be faced directly if one is to have any hope whatsoever of success. As the sages say, the only way to defeat a rhyming demon is to defuse his rhyme scheme. That was one thing about the sages, they always had a way with words. But then again, I suppose a rhyming demon needs a way with words as well. Thus do both sages and demons come under the scope of our discussion. Opposites attract, they say, and who could be more opposite than—"

"Fine!" Zimplitz broke in. "Your meaning is simple enough! We need a champion, to snatch Vushta back from the grasp of Guxx and the Netherhells!"

"Simple?" Snorphosio sniffed. "Nothing I ever say is ever simple, my good Zimplitz. You perhaps have not yet studied the ramifications of my ideas. That is the problem with you practical magicians, always leaping in before you fully weigh all the alternatives and—"

"Problem?" Zimplitz shrieked. "The only problem we have in this academy is those theoretical magicians who are so busy talking that they never get around to making any decisions, much less acting on them!"

There was a rumble in the distance, like thunder.

"Is it the Netherhells?" Zimplitz asked.

"Nonsense!" Snorphosio replied. "If it was, there would be a quake beneath our feet. Besides, this college is surrounded by a protective shell to ward off all demonic assaults. As all good theoretical magicians know—"

"Your pardon," Ebenezum interrupted, intent on defusing this argument before it got totally out of control. "If I might speak to you two gentlemen in private for a moment?"

My master would have this whole difficulty cleared up in a matter of minutes. But this exchange reminded me that I had a misunderstanding of my own that I had to straighten out. I turned to Norei, my beloved.

"Dearest," I whispered in her ear. "Might we also speak for a bit?"

She looked at me sternly. "Dearest?" she said rather more loudly than I might deem appropriate for a private conversation. "Aren't you getting the young women of your acquaintance confused? I would have thought, from your recent demonstration, that there is someone else who is the object of your affections!"

"Norei!" I cried. A number of others in the room had turned to stare at me. I lowered my voice to an urgent whisper. "Please! She was but a summer romance, long before we had met. We were trapped by the magic from the hat, and she panicked. Beyond that, she means little to me, and I mean nothing to her!"

"Wuntie?"

I jumped. Alea had walked up behind me as I had

earnestly engaged Norei in conversation. She wrapped both of her arms around one of mine. She frowned at Norei.

"Wuntie, dearest, is this young witch giving you trouble?"

"Wuntvor?" Norei stared dourly at Alea. "Are you telling me the truth about all this?"

"Yes!" I insisted. Wait a moment! Who was I answering?

"Uh, no!" I stammered. What was I saying? Why was Norei's breath so hot against my neck? Why did Alea have to stand so close? "Uh, I don't know!"

Both women looked at me wide-eyed, their faces a mixture of shock and anger. Both turned to leave.

"Wait . . ." I called. How could I get Norei to turn around? She shot me the slightest withering glance.

"Yes— I mean, uh . . ." I had trouble finding the exact words I needed. And Alea had turned around. She was walking back to me! Why did her blond curls have to shine so, even in this enclosed space?

"No, wait . . ." I began again.

Now Norei paused. She frowned in my direction.

"I mean . . ." My voice died out completely.

"Indeed," my master interrupted. "While I hate to intrude upon your good time, Wuntvor, we must get on with things. My fellow wizards have come to a decision. Zimplitz?"

"We have agreed," the other wizard began. "Rescuing Vushta is more important than our differences of approach to magic. Ebenezum is correct. We will do our best not to argue until our city is saved."

Zimplitz stepped back, yielding the floor to Snorphosio.

"Although my learned colleague and myself have some differences of opinion over the proper ordering of magic, we shall put our differences aside. While I am sure all the students and true magicians here realize that theoretical magic is the basis of all sorcerous thought, and without the development of theory there would be no advancement within the field and we should soon slip back to some dark age where we would forget all but the simplest spells, still, despite these many obvious and overwhelmingly far-reaching disadvantages . . ." Snorphosio's voice died in his throat as he saw the way my master was looking at him. The elder wizard coughed. "Rescuing Vushta is more important!"

"And"—Ebenezum's stern expression turned to a benevolent smile—"what else have we decided?"

Zimplitz once again stepped forward. "Both Snorphosio and myself have massive libraries of magical craft. We have yet to agree on what series of spells would be best to assure our victory over the Netherhells. However, we have agreed on one thing. What spells we use cannot be performed totally from a distance. One of our party must travel through the Netherhells until he finds whatever horrendous spot wherein the demons have hidden our beloved city. Once that person stands in the remains of Vushta, our spells will be complete."

Zimplitz took a deep breath. "In short, for our plans to succeed, we need a champion."

"Doom," Hendrek remarked.

"Oh, Wuntie!" Alea shivered at my side. "Into the Netherhells! How horrible!"

Norei allowed me an icy stare from where she stood some distance away.

"The Netherhells!" Snarks had sidled close to me. He pulled back enough of his voluminous hood to be understood. "I've always wanted to visit my homeland again. The sulfur pools! The boiling oil! The cries of the damned!" The demon used one edge of the hood to dab at the corners of his eyes. "I'm just a sentimental old fool!"

"And now," my master said, "we must choose our champion."

"It will not take long," Zimplitz added. "I sense that there is a bearer of great magic in our midst. Magic always lingers in the halls of this academy, but my years of training tell me there was an extraordinary burst of sorcery within these walls mere moments ago. And we will need an extraordinary man or woman as our champion. He or she must be brave and true, for, should he make a single false step in the Netherhells, he may be damned for all eternity."

Zimplitz lifted both hands high in the air. "The champion is among us! We have but to wait and we will be shown the way!"

The room was silent. I stared about the great hall of the academy, a bit in awe of all that must have happened here before, as well as what occurred now around me. Perhaps Zimplitz was right, and magic at this moment did fill the air. Who would be our champion? One of the professors? Tomm, or one of the other students? Or could it even be one of the band with which I had traveled from the Western Kingdoms?

I heard a rustling in the far distance. The hairs on the back of my neck tingled with anticipation. There was magic near!

The rustling grew louder, like a dozen tiny feet scrabbling on stone. It was coming from the direction of the library. All of us turned to see what magic might be revealed.

"Eep eep! Eep eep! Eep eep!" The three ferrets burst into the room as one, their red-brown forms streaking straight toward me.

"Our champion!" Zimplitz cried. "It is a sign!"

The three ferrets nuzzled against my legs.

"Ferrets?" Snarks murmured.

"Indeed. This is our champion." Ebenezum pulled at his beard. "Forgive me, Wuntvor, if I remark that you are not exactly what we originally had in mind."

"Agreed." Zimplitz nodded silently. "But you cannot deny that the magic was there. I think you sell your own apprentice short. With Vushta gone, we are woefully low on champions. He will have to do."

"Oh, Wuntie!" Alea exclaimed. "To the Netherhells?"

# FIVE

*Heroics can be costly and involve some degree of
personal danger for the participating wizard. But
for the truly resourceful magician, this does not
have to be! Consider the advantages of long-dis-
tance magic, by which you may gain all the publicity value and save all the expense. But, you say,
don't heroes have to be present at the battle? For
the properly prepared mage, nothing could be more
heroic than a well-timed combination of printed
handbills, subtly placed rumor, and perhaps a brief
personal appearance tour. Still expensive? Nonsense! Do you know how much a heroic wizard can
charge for personal appearances?*

—*from* Ebenezum the Wizard's Handy Pocket
Guide to Everyday Wizardry,
*fourth edition*

I was going to the Netherhells.

I looked down at the ferrets rubbing my legs. It all
seemed a bit unreal, as if I were taking part in some mid-
summer pageant and looked up to see snow on the trees.

In a way, I had been given a great honor. After all,
somebody had to do it. It would be better if I looked on
the bright side. Perhaps I would finally see the thousand
forbidden delights!

Snorphosio cleared his throat. "We probably have
not made all the ramifications of this choice clear, either
to the rest of our party here, or to our—er—champion." The aged professor waved vaguely in my direction. "You will not have to go alone on your quest, and
neither will you have to go unarmed. We will pick a
suitable companion or two from amidst our group to accompany you in your peril. All champions, of course,

need companions. It states so clearly in the *Hero's Guide to Weapons and Etiquette*. Page forty-three, I believe.''

Zimplitz seemed about to say something, but Snorphosio continued his speech rapidly, refusing to be interrupted. ''You will also be provided with weapons, magical weapons, the very best that can be found in the whole of''—Snorphosio paused again—''er—well, let's see what we have left in the basement, shall we?''

I had the feeling Snorphosio was speaking to instill confidence in me. For the moment, it did not seem to be working.

''Very good—'' Zimplitz began.

''And one more thing!'' Snorphosio shouted to override his fellow magician. ''We will of course provide you with certain spells and duties to perform once you have reached your goal, so that we can defeat the Netherhells forever. You will be informed as to the exact nature of these duties—er—once we ourselves determine what they are.''

''Indeed,'' Ebenezum said. ''I believe we all need to prepare. What say we gather together in this hall at sunset?''

All agreed to my master's plans and the various parties began to leave the hall, many with specific duties assigned by one or another of the three wizards.

For the first time I grew afraid. Would I be left all alone here on my last day on the surface?

One thing I determined: If I was going to go underground in a few brief hours, perhaps never to see the sun again, I wasn't going to spend the rest of my afternoon standing about inside the wizards' college. I strode briskly outside into the sunlight.

''Oh, Wuntie!'' Alea cried, her blond curls truly brilliant in the late summer sun. ''To the Netherhells?''

I silently wished she would stop saying that. It was bad enough that I had to go and be a hero. It would be infinitely worse if my last few hours on the surface were spent with people constantly reminding me of my heroism.

Hubert waved his top hat in my direction. " 'Tis a noble thing you do for us all," the dragon intoned. "We thought later this afternoon we might do a little something in your honor."

Alea jumped with glee. "That's right, Wuntie! A real send-off!"

A sudden chill ran down my spine. I whispered my reply: "You're not thinking of having another show, are you?"

"The very thing!" Hubert confirmed. "Alea, didn't I tell you this apprentice was a perceptive lad?"

"Oh, yes, Hubert." Alea was once again looking at me through half-closed lids. "And he's very good with animals, too."

Alea stepped close to me. "Oh, Wuntie!" she said, taking my hand. "Maybe we can sing a song just for you!"

"Yes!" the dragon cried. "A brilliant idea! We could call it 'The Ballad of Wuntvor'!"

Hubert sang the first few notes tentatively:

> Wuntvor the hero sure is swell,
> Went for us all down to the Netherhells . . .

Alea frowned. "That's not quite it. I think we need to develop his character a little at the beginning, and let the audience know exactly what kind of human being would go on such a hopeless quest. You know, like . . ." She began to sing in her clear, high soprano:

> Wuntvor was honest, couldn't be bought,
> Though he sometimes acted before he thought . . .

"Well, the pathos is nice," Hubert agreed, "but it's the blood and guts that always gets the audience!"

The dragon sang again:

> Wuntvor strode boldly, no fear in him,
> though the demons might tear him
> limb from limb . . .

I decided it was time to excuse myself. Although I was sure the two vaudevillians meant well, their attempts to honor me felt as reassuring as lying down for a nap and thereupon hearing someone read your eulogy. Perhaps I could find some quiet place in the sun where I might meditate.

"Wuntvor? May I talk to you?"

There, at the edge of a copse of trees, stood Norei.

I ran quickly across the intervening field. Had my beloved forgiven me at last? I took her hand and kissed her chastely upon the cheek.

Norei frowned. "Not in front of everyone, Wuntvor! I only wanted to talk to you for a moment!"

Norei looked at me with eyes the color of a forest glade, her perfect lips pressed into a perfect frown. Oh, how could I make her see that, compared to her, Alea was a rapidly fading memory!

"Norei—" I began.

"I don't want any excuses, Wuntvor." Her voice was grim. "I want the truth."

"The truth?" What was my beloved saying? "But I always tell—"

"Oh, yes, I know." Norei grimaced. Did I detect the slightest beginnings of a smile? "But you do sometimes tend to embellish here and there. It is part of your nature, I know, and I don't think you mean badly by it for the most part . . ."

I stepped closer to her, but she backed away.

"Now I'm trying to talk!" she exclaimed, her voice stern again. "After the things you've said to me, your recent actions with that—blond person—are very—unethical." She spoke haltingly, each word louder than the one before it, as if she could barely contain her anger.

She paused to stare at me. She bit her lip. When she spoke again, the words came quickly.

"Well, it's just that I may never see you again, so I thought I'd give you a chance to explain."

My heart leaped in my chest. So my beloved might forgive me after all! Quickly, but rationally, I tried to explain how I had discovered the chart, and the hat, and the flowers in my hand, and how, just at that moment, Alea had been passing by, and I had had a generous impulse, but had not made myself clear enough, so that Alea had come into the room instead of allowing me to give her the flowers through the window, and then the true nature of the hat had become apparent, and I, gentleman that I was, could not bring myself to remove Alea's hands from about my protective neck, even though she was strangling me, which was approximately the moment that Norei had chosen to enter the room.

I stopped, totally out of breath, and looked into her eyes.

"I understand," she said at last. "Well, actually, I don't understand, but the whole thing is so complex that I'm willing to give you the benefit of the doubt." She looked toward the wizards' college. "It's a bit too public out here, isn't it? Let's take a walk, back among the trees."

I did as Norei asked. Maybe there were some advantages to this hero business after all.

"Wuntvor?"

It was my master's voice! I took a sharp breath.

"Ebenezum is calling!" I whispered.

"Wuntvor?" His voice was much closer now.

"Perhaps you had better go," Norei whispered back.

"Wuntvor?" He was at the edge of the trees now.

"Perhaps I should," I replied. We did our best to rapidly disentangle ourselves. There seemed to be a problem. Somehow our shirts had gotten buttoned together.

"I shall remember this moment always," I said as I hastily attempted to unbutton and rebutton our respective shirts.

Norei glanced down at my handiwork. "At the rate you're going, this moment will never end. Here, let me do that." Her sure fingers had us free in no time.

I turned to go, but Norei's hand was on my neck. I glanced back at her, and her lips were touching mine. We kissed a final time.

"Wuntvor!" my beloved whispered. "Good luck!"

I managed somehow to crash my way out of the thicket and reach the spot where Ebenezum stood, calling my name.

There was a look of concern on the wizard's face. "Do you feel well, 'prentice? You appear somewhat dazed."

I assured him it was only a bit too much of the summer sun.

My master nodded soberly. "I can understand your need of it, going so soon to face the underworld. 'Tis a thing both noble and dangerous you are about to attempt, Wuntvor. And I am glad that you are the one who is going to attempt it."

Ebenezum paused a moment to stroke his beard, then spoke again. "I, who know you best of all our assembled company, believe that we have made the proper choice for our champion. We have been through a great deal together, Wuntvor, and, no matter what perils we have encountered, either singly or together, we have prevailed. You have a way, 'prentice, of seeming to invite disaster, and then at the last moment averting it. There are those in our company who might call it dumb luck, but I believe you have a unique magical gift!"

Ebenezum chuckled softly. "Anyone else playing with that hat would have produced rabbits. Only you, Wuntvor, could bring forth ferrets!"

I smiled along with my master. I had never quite

thought about my production of the ferrets in that way. Perhaps I did have a unique magical gift. I would march down into the Netherhells and bring Vushta back straightaway! With my master's faith behind me, how could I possibly fail?

"I have been talking with the other mages," Ebenezum continued, "and I think we have decided upon a very positive course of action. The other two are ironing out the fine points while I keep my distance." Ebenezum sniffed delicately. "I have not yet had time to discuss my malady in any great detail with either of these learned men. But, from what little discourse we have had, I believe there is hope of at least a temporary cure! Therefore, while the uncertainty of my condition prevents me from personally entering the Netherhells, I should be able to magically assist you on a regular basis from our temporary headquarters here at the wizards' college."

This was even better news. What could possibly go wrong now?

"Learned sirs!" someone called to us from the entranceway to the college. I turned to see Klothus waving in our direction. "Your wizardship! I have your new robes!"

"Ah, very good." Ebenezum patted at his mustache. "I have not felt very wizardly of late. At least now I can look the part."

I accompanied my master as we walked rapidly over to the royal costumer. How fine Ebenezum would look in brand-new robes of royal blue, tastefully inlaid with silver.

But my master's smile vanished as he approached. He grabbed the fabric in one trembling hand.

"What is the meaning of this?" he rumbled.

"What is the meaning of what?" Klothus replied. "I got what you needed, a new set of four-nineteens."

I looked carefully at the bit of cloth Ebenezum held in his trembling hands. It was midnight blue, but the tastefully inlaid silver pattern was not of moons and stars. It was, rather, tastefully inlaid with ducks and bunnies.

"Ducks and bunnies?" My master was truly enraged.

"Of course!" Klothus retorted. He squinted at the remnants of robe still on Ebenezum's body. "Oh dear, those are moons and stars, aren't they? That would be a four-seventeen, wouldn't it?" The costumer cleared his throat. "Well, it's a natural mistake."

"Natural?" My master sounded like there might be an earthquake beginning in his throat.

"Well," Klothus frowned, "is it my fault that you can't keep your clothes clean? I've been under a lot of stress, what with Vushta vanishing and all."

Ebenezum's shaking became more violent as he turned a very unattractive shade of white.

"You—" the wizard began.

"I see," Klothus remarked, somewhat taken aback. He continued rapidly. "It's an awfully popular number—"

"—call yourself—" The wizard's voice was rising. It seemed to hold a hint of winter storm.

"—and the costume shop here is not as well stocked as the main branch—well, what used to be the main branch." Klothus had begun to edge away from my master.

"A costumer?" Ebenezum's voice was approaching full gale.

"Still," Klothus called over his shoulder as he ran away, "I'll see what I can do."

My master shuddered and took a deep breath. "Yes," Ebenezum said slowly. "Indeed. See what you can do."

But by then Klothus was lost in the distance.

Ebenezum turned back to me. "Sometimes it is the day-to-day problems that wear you down the most. Still, when you return, all this should be behind us. If I have not found a permanent cure already, one will surely be forthcoming with all the might of Vushta returned to us. And, once I am able to again use magic to my fullest powers, we will begin your wizardly training in earnest!"

Ebenezum looked at the sky. "There are still a few more minutes before sunset. I must return inside and consult with my fellow mages. I shall see you there soon enough." With that, the sorcerer spun about and walked rapidly back into the college.

So I was alone again, to silently witness the last few minutes of a late summer's afternoon. The wind shifted, carrying the singing voices of Hubert and Alea.

"No, no!" Alea cried. "We still need to personalize the danger!" She sang again:

> Wuntvor was young and not too discreet,
> And when he walked he had two left feet!

"No, you are wrong!" Hubert retorted. "We must stress the danger of his mission if we are to keep audiences interested!" The dragon's voice boomed:

> Wuntvor the hero can't be a dud,
> For the demons will then drink his blood.
> They'll tear him apart with hideous groans,
> And pick bits of him from their teeth with his bones!

"Hey," Alea admitted grudgingly, "that's pretty good. Yes, we'll put that in for sure!"

*Pick their teeth with my bones?* I tried to swallow, but my mouth was suddenly far too dry. I decided that I should walk in some direction where the wind could not possibly carry Alea's and Hubert's voices to me.

I made my way back through the copse of trees. Snarks and Hendrek stood in the shade at the far side.

"Wuntvor," Snarks remarked. "You appear a little green. Still, you're going to have to do better than that if you really want to imitate demonic coloration."

I smiled halfheartedly at Snark's comment. My mind was elsewhere. *With my bones?*

"Doom," Hendrek added.

No, I thought to myself, not if I could help it. I took a deep breath. Ebenezum had often told me that the difference between a good magician and a bad one was the magician's attitude. Well, I was determined to have the best attitude possible under the circumstances.

I thought for a moment about Snarks's remark.

"Should I attempt to imitate demonic coloration?"

"Actually, I don't think that is at all necessary," Snarks replied. "Things are changing in the Netherhells these days, you know. It is not the barbaric place it once was."

"Really?" I said. Hearing Snarks speak reasonably about the place of his birth reassured me tremendously. Perhaps, I thought, I should find out a little more. "Is it safe then for humans to walk among demonkind?"

"Oh, without a doubt!" Snarks chuckled. "Provided, of course, you have a reasonable story for being in the Netherhells. In the last couple years I was there, they were establishing regular human-demon trade routes. I imagine by now that that commerce is even more highly developed."

"Then," I asked hopefully, "demons don't really eat humans?"

Snarks chuckled at my naiveté. "On the contrary, demons eat humans all the time! But don't worry, you are perfectly safe as long as you can show the demons you have a reason not to be eaten!"

"Oh," I replied. This was not as reassuring as I had hoped. Still, there was one more question I had to ask. "Then do demons really rip you apart and drink your blood?"

Snarks shook his head sadly. "Another example of negative demonic stereotyping! True, human ripping and blood drinking used to be big problems in the past. But now"—Snarks gave a dismissive wave of his hand —"in the course of regular human-demon encounters, I don't imagine that sort of thing happens more than once out of every five meetings."

"Once in five?" I asked.

Snarks nodded. "Of course, the statistics are a little higher in summer or around festival time. But what are a couple of humans more or less to the Netherhells? So, as you see, you can come and go as you please!"

"Oh," I answered. I decided not to ask him how demons picked their teeth. I sighed at some length and sat down beside them.

Snarks looked at me with some consternation.

"That's the problem with humans," he began. "They really never plan anything out in demonic detail. It's really too bad I can't go with you to show you the place. But I have been banished. If I were to return . . ." The demon shuddered. "Well, what they would do to me would make this college look tasteful!"

"Doom," Hendrek agreed. "I have much the same problem. If I were to go to the Netherhells, I should be beset by demons demanding hellish payment for my weapon. We would be stopped before we had even begun."

I nodded glumly. There seemed to be no escaping it. Whatever terrors I would have to face in the Netherhells, I would have to face them alone.

"Doom," Hendrek commented. "The sunset is the color of blood."

I turned to see where the warrior pointed his doomed club. He was right. The sky at the edge of the valley was a brilliant crimson tinged with orange. It was quite beautiful, really.

I also realized it might be the last sunset I would ever see.

# SIX

*Q:   And how do professional wizards cope with
stress?*

*A:   Stress? The real wizard doesn't even recog-
nize the meaning of the word. Why are you still
asking me questions? Can't you see I'm busy? This
spell is two days overdue! You're sitting on my ref-
erence books!*

   —*from* "A Conversation with Ebenezum, Greatest
      Wizard in the Western Kingdoms," *Wizard's
                              Quarterly, Vol. 4,
                                   No. 4 (Spring)*

The sky was rapidly darkening. The time had come to
go inside and face the collective wisdom of the three
mages.

   I must admit that there was a part of me that did not
want to go, what with the demons that made odd use of
your bones and all. But the fate, not only of Vushta and
my master, but of the entire world, depended on the
success of my mission. And that was an even more so-
bering thought. All in all, I was probably much better
off worrying about demonic dental habits.

   Still, I thought of Ebenezum's words as I approached
the Great Hall of the wizards' college. He had thought I
had some extra quality that always let me succeed, no
matter what the odds. It made me feel proud to know
that my master had such faith in me. And I knew I
would do everything possible to justify that faith.

   Snarks and Hendrek walked close behind me and I
saw the others of our party also gathering about the college. I knew all would be present for the final moment
of decision.

   The wizard students had placed large torches on

either side of the foyer and around the perimeter of the
Great Hall. They also had opened a window at hall's
end large enough for Hubert to put his head through
and watch the proceedings. This extra opening seemed
to have made the large room particularly drafty, for the
torches flared and guttered and gave everyone in the
room a dozen dancing shadows.

A cheer went up as I entered the room. I couldn't help
but smile. If fame was so wonderful now, how magnificent it would be when I was a full-fledged wizard!

"Welcome!" Zimplitz cried from where he stood on
the marble dais. "Now that the most important member
of our little band is here, we can make our final plans!"

There was some polite applause, led by Zimplitz
along with Ebenezum and Snorphosio, who stood
slightly behind the other wizards on the raised platform.

"Indeed." Ebenezum stepped forward. "The three of
us have conferred at some length as to the best plan to
follow for the rescue of Vushta. However, our discus-
sions are not so final that we do not still solicit your
help. If any of you assembled here find that you have
any questions or comments about any of our plans, we
will be glad to give you the floor for as long as you feel
necessary." My master looked at me. "And that applies
doubly to our young champion, Wuntvor the Apprentice!"

There was another brief cheer. Perhaps I was expected to say something now. To all these people, at the
same time? For the first time since I was given this
honor, I began to sweat. It seemed only natural that, if I
was about to go off and face the Netherhells, I should
be able to gather enough courage to address this assembly. Yes, now was the time. My master had given me
an opportunity to reply, and I was their champion, after
all. I took a deep breath and swallowed.

"Well—" I began.

"Of course," Snorphosio said over my hesitant voice,
"we do not have time for too much discussion. As my
colleagues have impressed upon me, now is the time for

action! Of course, action without proper discussion is often meaningless, as discussion without action sometimes lacks meaning as well, especially for those acting, not to mention those acted upon. But what happens when meaningless action is discussed—"

"Indeed!" Ebenezum interrupted. "I believe it is time we began our business. We must discuss three things this evening: the nature of your quest; your companions; and your magic weapons." He motioned to Zimplitz. "First, the weapons!"

Zimplitz pulled a sack from the back of the dais. "Come forward, Wuntvor," he called, "and I shall explain the nature of each of these three magic charms!"

As I approached, he reached into the sack and pulled forth a golden horn.

"This," Zimplitz intoned, "is Wonk, the Horn of Persuasion." He handed the golden instrument to me. "One blast upon this mighty horn and even the foulest demon will do your will."

The horn was cool in my hands. I held it up closer to the torchlight to examine the fine scrollwork etched into its handle.

"There is but one precaution I would ask of you," Zimplitz continued. "Whatever you do—"

I took a deep breath and blew.

Every man, woman, and mythological beast screamed and covered their ears as one.

"All right!" Zimplitz cried. "All right! You can do whatever you want!" His hands shook as he removed them from his ears. "But please don't blow it again!"

The audience before me murmured in all too ready agreement. I gingerly laid the horn on the edge of the platform before me.

"Next," Zimplitz continued, doing his best to regain his composure, "we have a very special sword."

He reached into the bag and pulled forth a silver sword in a scabbard of midnight blue, close in color to my master's robes when they were still clean and whole.

I took the weapon in both my hands. I touched the ornate silver hilt tentatively.

"May I?" I asked.

"Why of course!" Zimplitz replied. "There's no problem at all—uh—with taking out the sword."

Gently, I drew forth a length of highly polished steel.

"Hello," the sword said.

I almost dropped it. No one had told me this sword was going to talk!

"I hate to ask this," the sword continued, "but are you drawing me out of my scabbard for any particular reason?"

I shrugged. "At the moment, no," I replied, doing my best to keep up my end of the conversation. "Just wanted to get introduced."

The sword emitted a low whistle. "That's a relief, may I tell you! Very pleased to meet you! My name is Cuthbert!"

I introduced myself in turn, and told the sword we were going to go on an adventure together.

"Oh," Cuthbert replied with very little enthusiasm. "I don't—ahem—have to kill anybody, do I?"

I was rather taken aback. I told Cuthbert I really didn't know.

"Drat!" the sword cursed. "I just hate drawing blood. It gets me all splattered, and it's even worse if the mess dries. And let me tell you what happens if I hit bone! I mean, it can dull my blade in no time. And the noise people make! All that shrieking and grunting and crying. I tell you, it's enough to make me want to go into another line of work!"

"Excuse me," Zimplitz said, "but I think it's time for Cuthbert to go back into his scabbard."

I slid the sword back into its midnight-blue casing.

"Cuthbert is a bit of a coward, I'm afraid," Zimplitz remarked. "Luckily, we have no such problem with the third charm." Zimplitz put the bag down and reached into his pocket. He pulled out a small, red card and handed it to me, saying, "You never know when this will come in handy."

I stepped back a few feet to better read the card in the torchlight. There, printed in block letters, were the words GET OUT OF JAIL FREE.

I looked questioningly at the wizard.

"Put it in a pocket where it will be safe," was all Zimplitz said. "And now on to the choice of companions!"

This seemed to rouse the crowd again, which had been a little subdued ever since my experiment with Wonk.

"We considered a number of different methods of choosing suitable companions: a contest of valor; whoever picked the short straw; a study of possible royal blood in someone's lineage; one potato, two potato; but none of them suited all our needs until Ebenezum hit upon the scheme of complementary companions."

"Indeed." My master stepped forward again. "In order that we might best choose companions, I need to speak with certain of our number. Hendrek, step forth!"

"Doom!" The large warrior shuffled out of the crowd.

"We all have reasons for being here tonight. All of us, of course, wish to rescue Vushta and defeat the Netherhells! But some of us have more personal and more urgent reasons for coming here."

"Doom!" Hendrek agreed.

"Hendrek, unsheath your club from its restraining sack," my master instructed.

The large warrior looked questioningly at my master for an instant. Ebenezum nodded and Hendrek brought forth Headbasher.

"As you see, much of my malady has been brought under control," my master proclaimed. "Thanks to a series of simple remedial spells that Zimplitz located in one of his tomes, I am able to remain in the presence of modest magic with naught but a slight nasal drip." He paused to blow his nose. "Snorphosio has studied the spells already worked upon me and believes they have theoretical possibilities that may eventually lead to a total cure. Therefore, although I am still incapable of setting foot in the Netherhells, I should be able to fully participate in the above-ground operations."

So my master was on the way to a complete cure! I found my face had broken out into a smile. For the moment, I didn't even care that I faced imminent death.

"But, if I supervise the operations above ground," my master continued, "who will accompany Wuntvor to protect him from the dangers down below? It is a thorny problem."

"Doom," Hendrek concurred. He tentatively swung Headbasher above his head. The torchlight sputtered in the sudden breeze.

"It is especially difficult for you, for should the demons take over the surface world, they would demand payment for your cursed club and you would be forced to do their fiendish bidding."

"Doom," Hendrek remarked once again.

"Unless, of course," my master continued, "the spell we three wizards have been working on can sufficiently mask the true nature of your weapon from demonkind!"

"Doom?" Hendrek inquired.

"Then you could join Wuntvor on his trip to the Netherhells and add your might to our quest to save the surface world. It is your only chance, for, should the demons take the surface world, all wizards would be surely killed and any spell we concocted for you would quickly become null and void!"

Hendrek stared at his warclub for a long moment as if deep in thought, then, with a grunt, smashed Headbasher to the floor.

"Doom!" the large warrior cried.

"Good!" Ebenezum replied. "We have our first volunteer!"

Snarks was at my side. "I never cease to marvel at

how good your master is at talking, especially for a human being. Of course, being raised with demons, I am immune to most forms of verbal persuasion."

"Now," Ebenezum called. "I must talk to the demon Snarks. No, no, don't replace your hood. I am quite capable of talking with you now." My master blew his nose again.

Snarks strode up to the edge of the dais. "So at last we can talk face to face? What a relief. You can't believe how many things I've been meaning to tell you. About your costume—"

"That is being attended to." Ebenezum pulled at his beard. "I'm afraid I have some questions to ask you as well. You are a demon and thus have not formed the fears the rest of us have concerning the Netherhells."

"Perfectly true. Now I wanted to mention a little something about the way you sneeze—"

"That is being attended to as well," Ebenezum replied. "And yet you were banished from the Netherhells. What do you think will happen when the Netherhells take over the surface world?"

Snarks hesitated for a moment. "Well, demonkind doesn't bear me any great ill will, as long as I keep completely out of their sight. The way I figure it, if they didn't kill me before, I see no reason for them to kill me now. They will simply kick me out of the surface world."

"And where will you go?"

Snarks was temporarily speechless.

"Therefore," my master added quickly, "you must accompany Wuntvor and provide him with the necessary knowledge of the Netherhells."

"I must." Snarks nodded slowly. "Now let me give you a little advice about your hand gestures—"

"We have our second volunteer!" Ebenezum cried.

"Doom," Hendrek put in for emphasis.

"Now," my master added, "we must talk about our plan."

"A moment!" my beloved Norei interrupted. "Are there to be no more volunteers?"

"Indeed," my master replied. "I am afraid not. Two is all we can afford."

"But shouldn't an experienced magician accompany them?"

"Ideally, yes. Unfortunately, there are too few of us here to make use of any ideal plans. Wuntvor has performed magic before. He will be given a basic spell to help him complete his quest. That, plus his weapons and companions, must be enough to see him through."

Norei glanced at me, her deep green eyes filled with concern. She turned back to my master. "Why can't I go?"

Ebenezum again pulled at his beard. "Because we need you here. We have scoured the countryside and been unable to find even a dozen wizards. Now my companions here believe that there are still another half dozen mages hiding in the vicinity who may reveal themselves once our sorcery becomes evident. In addition, we will place a magical call to bring what rural wizards we can to join us, but our time is limited. The Netherhells have already struck once. We have no idea when they will strike again."

Norei still looked doubtful.

"You must join us!" Tomm the former tinker cried. "We will need your woods-trained senses in the battle to come. I look forward to working side by side with you, and trading bits of magic lore."

Trading bits of magic lore? Who was this big ox kidding? How dare he smile at my beloved that way? I knew the sort of things a lummox like that wanted to trade, and I didn't like it one bit!

"I am afraid," Ebenezum interjected before Norei could speak again, "that you will have to stay and give your fellow magicians a hand. We have no time to make any other changes in our plans."

There was a tremendous crash. The room shook once,

tossing all those standing to the floor. It was as if the earth heard my master's remark and felt the need to reinforce it.

"Is it the Netherhells?" Ebenezum asked the others.

"The possibility exists," Snorphosio agreed. "Although this college is surrounded by a protective shell that is meant to insure it against demonic assault. Although, come to think of it, the entire metropolis of Vushta was surrounded by a protective shell as well—"

"We may have taken too long with our plans!" my master cried. "Hubert! Quickly! Go and scout the area!"

"What?" Alea cried as the dragon departed. "Does this mean we don't get to do our song?"

Ebenezum shook his head. "Indeed. There is no time."

"And we worked so long on it!" Alea sighed. "We decided at last on a traditional ballad about the death of heroes. It had such a wonderfully mournful quality."

"Indeed." My master had already turned his attention to me. "Listen carefully, for any word I say might be my last. You have seen how the horn works. The sword not only talks, but is capable of communication with us at the college. That is, if the college still exists. As to the card, well, Zimplitz thought it might be of some use."

"It was the best we could do on short notice!" Zimplitz interjected. "Our magical weapons storeroom is almost as bad as our library."

"Be that as it may," Ebenezum continued, "I have written down on this scrap of paper the one spell you need. Memorize it at your first convenience. Now you must go to the very heart of the Netherhells, for that is where they have hidden Vushta. And it is in Vushta that you will find the only one who can effect a cure: Guxx Unfufadoo!"

"Guxx?" I whispered. I would have to face the dreaded rhyming demon.

Ebenezum nodded grimly. "The other wizards have determined that all we have experienced is somehow intertwined: my malady, the overabundance of magic in the land, and the disappearance of Vushta. To cure all three, and to stop the Netherhells from making any further gains, you must enter Vushta and get one thing, and one thing only, from the demon Guxx."

Only one!? I tried to find hope within my breast. I had been given weapons, companions, and a special spell. With luck, and the proper strategy, it might be possible. Snarks and Hendrek pressed close to me on either side. I looked up to my master.

"What," I whispered, "do I need to take from the demon Guxx?"

Ebenezum stared deep within my eyes. "A single nose hair," was his reply.

"Doom," Hendrek observed.

And then the earth really began to shake.

# SEVEN

*Wizards are constantly subject to negative publicity. A case in point: One elderly wizard of my acquaintance, whenever he was bothered by unexpected guests, would immediately cast one of three spells upon them, either turning them to stone, transforming them into segmented worms, or blasting them entirely out of the kingdom. Now, some wrong-headed do-gooders, hearing about the aged mage's predilections, formed an angry torch-bearing mob, forcing the now wronged wizard to flee to a distant kingdom altogether. How much better it would have been if the aged wizard had thought to inform the populace of the true benefits of the spells he used on those who came to bother him! For example, those people who have experienced it will tell you that nothing is more restful than being turned to stone, while transformation into a worm brings you closer to the earth. As to being totally blasted from the wizard's domain, I challenge you: Can you think of any other way you can travel such a great distance for free?*

—*from* The Teachings of Ebenezum,
*Volume XVI*

It happened in an instant. Where once there was a floor of solid stone, now there was a gaping hole. Something small and sickly yellow in color leaped from the hole into the great hall. And that something was wearing a loud blue-and-orange checked suit.

"Greetings from the Netherhells!" Brax the Sales-demon cried.

"Doom!" The mighty Hendrek was the first into the fray, moving with amazing speed for one so large. But then Brax was his personal demon.

"How you doing, Hendy baby!" the salesdemon said. "I have just a minute here before the battle really gets under way, and I want to make a request. As you no doubt realize, you're way behind on your rental payments for the cursed club Headbasher. I've done what I can to keep the powers that be from demanding the final payment, but i'm afraid your credit rating is not very pretty. Still, I've been authorized to give you one more chance. All you have to do is make one large payment right now and the contract will be considered paid to date!" The demon nimbly dodged the warclub's swing. "That's right! All you have to do to return to the good graces of the most fearsome creditors in the Netherhells is to hand over Ebenezum the Wizard!"

"Doom!" Hendrek swung his club again.

"My good warrior!" There seemed to be an edge in the demon's voice. "Be reasonable here! How can we strike fear into the masses, not to mention damning souls for all eternity, if our customers won't cooperate? Surely you can see my point of view!"

"Doom!" Headbasher crashed into the stones where Brax had stood but a second before.

Brax waved both hands in the air. "Well, what can I do? My hands are tied. We will simply have to take Ebenezum anyway, with no credit to your account!" The demon whistled. "Bring on the Dread Collectors!"

I felt as if my veins had turned to ice. We had only seen the Dread Collectors once before, but I remembered them all too well. I especially remembered their many claws, their even greater number of teeth, and the relentless ferocity with which they attacked.

This time they seemed even more horrible than before.

They burst from the hole in the floor.

It is difficult to describe the Collectors, for they move so fast you can never quite make out their exact shape. There appeared to be three of them, and all they did was slash and bite and try to rip out your neck. They moved as fast as Hendrek under the enchantment of his club. Whenever you turned around, they were there.

The last time we had seen these fiends, it was but for an instant. This time, it would be far worse. As they approached, I realized there was a pattern to their growling, mewling, squealing voices. After a fashion, they actually spoke!

The three things swept across the floor in our direction and all three spoke as one.

"We come for payment!" the Collectors growled.

All around me, I saw my companions readying for battle. I vowed that I would do the best I could as well, though I had but a stout oak staff to protect myself.

But wait! No longer did I have to defend myself with only my stout oak staff. I had been given weapons —magic weapons! Quickly, I reached for the midnight-blue scabbard. I leaped toward the nearest Collector. With a blood cry on my lips, I drew forth Cuthbert, the enchanted sword.

"Wait a minute!" the sword cried.

I stumbled midlunge. It was somewhat disconcerting to be in battle and have your weapon talk to you. I lost my balance and fell by the feet of the nearest fiend. The Collector's claws raked the air above my head.

The sword screeched against stone as I fell. The Collector reared back at the noise. I scrambled quickly to my feet.

"Really!" the sword continued. "Do you think this is such a good idea?"

I swung the sword toward a rapidly retreating Collector. "I do not think"—I managed between lunges— "that this is the best time—for a conversation."

"I could not disagree more!" the sword retorted. "I mean, have you exhausted all the other possibilities? You'd be surprised how many times a conversation between adversaries, even a very short one, can prevent a—*yelp!*"

The sword connected with the Collector as the fearsome beast spun away. I pulled the blade free of the matted mass. The shining steel was covered by an ichorous green.

"Do you see what happens when you start fighting?" the sword complained. "I mean, green ichor! Do you know how long it takes to clean off green ichor?"

The Dread Collectors had once again retreated to their fearsome formation. So we had somehow repulsed the first attack. But then they growled and came for us twice as fast.

"We come for blood!" the Collectors snarled as one.

One of the things was heading straight for me.

"See what you've gotten us into?" the sword remarked.

I ignored the weapon's prattle and quickly stepped aside. But I had expected to find a bare spot on the floor on which to stand. Instead, I encountered all-too-solid flesh.

"Doo-*oof!*" Hendrek cried as we collided. Both of us lost our footing simultaneously.

Two sets of Dread Collectors' claws raked the air above our heads, digging deep into each other's pelts. Their screams were deafening. There was green ichor everywhere.

I rolled away from the still interlocked Collectors and regained my feet in front of the dais. I took a moment to catch my breath and see where next I could use my sword.

The student wizards and Hubert seemed to have joined together to keep the third collector at bay with a combination of well hurled paving stones and dragon fire. Snorphosio and Zimplitz had used the extra moments during which the rest of us had been fighting the Collectors to each develop a counter spell. Zimplitz's enchantment was a bright red hammer that smashed to the floor whenever a Collector was near, while Snorphosio had devised a delicate weblike thing that didn't quite seem to work as of yet. Snorphosio cursed as a second Collector passed through the device without apparent harm, then shouted another quick spell, which apparently had no further effect whatsoever.

And what of my beloved? Norei was at the other end of the dais, using her spells to fight off Brax the Salesdemon, who appeared to be brandishing one of his enchanted daggers.

"No!" I cried. I rushed forward, intent on rescuing her from her peril.

I felt something strange brush against my chest. Was this some other insidious form of demon magic? I quickly reached inside my shirt and pulled forth a single flower. The delicate stem felt cold between my fingers. I remembered Norei's warning about excess magic bringing back the spells! I tossed the flower away as I ran for my beloved. I definitely would have to get rid of the pieces of that hat at the first opportunity!

And then I heard the sound which I had dreaded most. My master had begun to sneeze.

Even with Zimplitz's cure, then, the magic here was too much for him. Little wonder, with a pair of spells and half a dozen fantastic creatures in the room. But that meant that he was totally defenseless!

I then made one of the most difficult decisions of my young life. Norei was capable of holding her own. I must protect my master! I leaped to the top of the dais and turned toward the battle on the floor, sword at the ready.

I had acted none too soon. All three Collectors, sensing my master's weakness, had disengaged from their other battles to attack him as one!

"We want the wizard!" the Collectors roared together.

But there was another noise as well, like the scrambling of many tiny feet across a floor of stone. An instant before I saw them, I heard their familiar cry:

"Eep eep! Eep eep! Eep eep!"

And the three ferrets jumped upon the lead Collector.

It was an unequal fight at best, but it made me proud to see those ferrets attempt the impossible; boldly giving their lives to protect me, no doubt, the person who gave them life upon this earth.

"Violence always ends this way," the sword muttered. "Mark my words. If you play around, you're going to get hurt!"

I ignored the whining weapon and shifted my position, sword forward, back to the wall. Thanks to the ferrets, I was as prepared as I could be for the Collectors' worst assault. They would surely kill me, but maybe I could take one of the fiends along.

"We will not be stopped!"

The lead monster shook my tiny allies across the room.

The ferrets dispensed with, the Collectors continued their headlong charge. I braced myself, knowing that in a moment it would all be done.

Ebenezum sneezed.

Thankfully, I had repositioned myself slightly to one side of the great wizard and thus was spared the main force of the blow. The Dread Collectors were not so lucky. The full extent of my master's nasal effluvium sprayed mightily upon them.

The dread fiends stopped dead in their tracks.

"We don't like getting wet!" the Collectors yelped as one.

"Now we will take the upper hand!" I cried.

"Are you so su—" my weapon began. But I sheathed the offending sword before it could complete its sentence. I had more than one enchantment up my sleeve. I knelt quickly and reached into the sack on the dais's edge.

"Hurry, Collectors!" Brax called from where he still dealt with Norei. "Guxx is expecting us!"

It was Guxx then, behind the attack? I could no longer hesitate. I drew forth the horn of persuasion.

I took a deep breath.

And I blew.

I blew mightily upon Wonk. Everyone screamed and covered their ears.

"Must you?" Brax said with some irritation. "Oh, very well. We'll take this one instead."

The salesdemon nodded once and a pair of Dread Collectors grasped Norei's arms. They rushed away, back to the hole from which they had erupted.

"Wuntvor!" Norei screamed as she was lost from sight.

Brax shrugged. "I can't go back empty-handed." And he jumped in the hole after the others.

I stared for a moment, stunned, at the last place I had seen my beloved.

"Doom," Hendrek commented as he appeared at my side.

"I must go after her," was all I could say.

"She is a qualified witch!" Snorphosio reminded me. "With luck she will survive. You need to know more about your weapons, and the spell we will use—"

"I must rescue her," I cut in. I had no more time for theory.

"But Wuntie!" Alea called from where she had cowered in the corner of the room. "You look as if the battle has exhausted you! You must rest first! I can help you relax!"

I shook my head. "I must follow her." I swallowed, but my throat was still far too dry. "Now."

Ebenezum blew his nose mightily.

"Indeed! Let the lad go! But remember, Wuntvor, you must rescue Vushta as well. Until the kingdom is once again whole, they may come and snatch any one of us, at any time!"

"I'll remember, master!" I gathered up my magical weapons. I wore Cuthbert at my belt and carried a sack filled with Wonk over my shoulder.

"Hendrek!" I called. "Snarks! Are you coming?"

"Doom!" Hendrek said at my side. The cursed club

Headbasher quivered in his enormous hand.

"I'm coming! I'm coming!" Snarks cried, tying his monastic robes tight about his small form. "That's the problem with humans. All these last-minute decisions!"

I waved a final time to my master. With Snarks and Hendrek behind me, I began my descent into the Netherhells.

# EIGHT

*And what do you do if you come upon a dark cave? Then the knowledgeable wizard would say: "Into darkness, let there be light." And the truly knowledgeable wizard would add: "Let there also be cheese, bread, fresh vegetables, plenteous members of the opposite sex, and enough mead to make it a thoroughly enjoyable weekend!"*

—*from* Thirty Days to Better Wizardry *by Ebenezum, Greatest Wizard in the Western Kingdoms, fourth edition.*

There was nothing but darkness.

Something bumped into me.

"Doom," came a voice behind me.

"Hey, watch your feet! Just like humans! Didn't anybody think enough to bring a light?" a second voice complained.

"Zrrrmmmnn," a third voice mumbled. For a minute, I thought Snarks had hidden himself again beneath his hood. But then I realized I had just heard him speak. Who else was here with us?

"Hendrek?" I called. "Snarks? Is there anyone else around?"

"How could you tell?" Snarks retorted.

"Doom," Hendrek added.

"Ouch!" Snarks cried. "Watch where you swing that club, will you?"

"If we don't stay together, we're going to get lost," Hendrek stated.

"Hey," Snarks replied. "I'm never going to get lost here. The Netherhells is my home turf!"

"Grrffmmm!" the other voice mumbled with some urgency.

"Wait!" I insisted. "Don't you two hear something?"

"Only the labored breathing of this out-of-condition warrior. And after all the diet plans I've suggested!"

"Doom! It was lucky for all of us that I thought to bring food with us. The wizards, you know, had put some provisions in a second sack."

"Wait a second," Snarks interjected. "You didn't need to bring any food! Demons have to eat, too, you know. It would probably do both of you some good to sample some Netherhells delicacies. Like sweet demon pie! Ah, there's a dish! Of course, you have to be careful! Those brambles can really stick to your gums!"

I felt something banging at my hip.

"Crffllvvmm!" the muffled voice cried with frustration.

"No!" I repeated. "Wait! I'm sure there's another sentient being here!"

"I'm not all that sure how many sentient beings are here already," Snarks added.

"Doom." I felt Hendrek's great bulk bump against my back.

"Would you keep off my feet!" Snarks screamed. "I should be leading the way, anyways. I'm the demon here!"

"Grrjjfflblltmm!" the voice mumbled in earnest.

"There!" I said in triumph. "Didn't you hear that?"

"Oh, that!" Snarks replied. "I just thought Hendrek had indigestion."

The beating on my leg redoubled.

"It's the sword!" I exclaimed as I suddenly realized the source of the sound.

"What's the sword?" Snarks began. But he fell silent when I drew my weapon from its scabbard.

Cuthbert glowed with a blinding light.

"Well, it's about time," the sword said haughtily. "Here I am, shouting my head off, and no one's paying the slightest bit of attention to me!"

"We didn't know," I answered, shielding my eyes

from the sword's blinding intensity. "We could hardly hear you at all."

"Oh, it's that nasty scabbard again!" Cuthbert complained. "It's so dark and close in there. No ventilation whatsoever! But it's what I have to call home now, isn't it?"

"Still," I remarked, doing my best to change the subject, "I'm glad I pulled you out so you can glow. I never imagined you could do that!"

"Well, that's what I was trying to tell you all along. Of course I can glow! I'm a magic sword, aren't I?"

"Up until now," Snarks interjected, "all your magic has been in your mouth." The demon looked away from Cuthbert's blinding light. "Say, couldn't you tone down your brightness a little bit?"

"I'm doing my best," the sword huffed. "Still, my light would be much better if I wasn't coated with green ichor."

"Doom," Hendrek responded. "It is a weapon's lot to be coated with the results of battle."

"And that's the problem, isn't it?" Cuthbert said. "I didn't ask to be a sword, now did I? Why couldn't I have been a magic mirror? I would have been perfectly happy, lying to people about who was the fairest in the land. But no, those magicians needed a sword, so—"

"Excuse me," I interrupted, "but hadn't we better be getting on with our quest? I mean, the woman we're trying to rescue may have been dragged halfway through the Netherhells by now."

"Doom." Hendrek nodded grimly.

"You know, folks, we could go back up to the surface. Then I wouldn't have to glow at all. We could just sit around and talk in natural light!"

"Let's get this over with," Snarks agreed. "I don't mind this sword giving us light, but does it have to talk, too?"

"Oh, dear," Cuthbert said. "You really don't want to listen, do you?"

"Let's look at it this way," Snarks replied. "Who

wants to take advice from a sword?"

"My point exactly!" Cuthbert exclaimed. "But now, what if I was a magic mirror? You'd certainly take advice from a magic mirror!"

I lifted Cuthbert before me and led the way down the tunnel to the Netherhells.

"Does any of this look familiar yet?" I asked Snarks.

"Nothing I recognize," the demon answered. "I believe we're still in the access tunnel. They build these things all the time to perform some bit of mischief or other on the surface. I'm surprised sometimes, with all this tunneling going on, that bits of the surface world don't come crashing in on top of the demons' heads."

"Doom," Hendrek said. "Perhaps it has."

I was struck by the warrior's thought. "Do you mean Vushta might have fallen through by accident?"

"Where would demons be more likely to perform mischief than in the city of a thousand forbidden delights? Doom!"

"Hmmm," Snarks mused. "There is truth in what you say. Still, I prefer to think the demons built their tunnels to sink Vushta by design rather than accident. It's that old Netherhells pride, you know."

"Doom!" Hendrek responded.

My eyes were at last adjusting to the light from the magic sword. The tunnel we traversed seemed to be carved out of solid rock. I did my best not to think of how much power it would take to make a tunnel like this. Or how much magic.

Cuthbert whistled. "This place does go on, doesn't it? That's one thing about being a magic sword. You sure get out a lot. I've seen places I would never have imagined when I was but a small spell on some magician's lips. I should look on the bright side more often. Magic mirrors get stuck in one spot, you know. All they ever get to do is hang around all day long."

Cuthbert sighed. "If only I didn't have to kill people. It's almost always a mess, let me tell you. And their death screams get on my nerves!"

"Could you shut up for a minute and turn your glow down?" Snarks asked. "I think I see some faint light up ahead."

"I do all this work for you, and this is the thanks I get!" Cuthbert complained. "Well, if that's all the use you have for me, why don't you just put me back in the scabbard, then?"

I did as the sword suggested. The weapon's complaints were muffled by its midnight-blue sheath.

Snarks had been right. There was a light ahead, faint compared to the blinding glow of the sword, and a little greenish in color.

"Now!" Snarks said with some satisfaction. "We are approaching the real Netherhells!"

I let my hand rest on my sword hilt. Somehow, descending through the tunnel, we had seemed distanced from both the surface and the hells below, somehow separated from our quest. Soon we would see the real Netherhells, filled with the real demons. The question was: Would the real demons let us pass?

"Snarks?" I asked. "Should we be prepared for trouble?"

"Not necessarily," the demon reassured me. "It depends in what sector of the Netherhells we find ourselves at tunnel's end. Once I see the vista before me, I shall know in an instant what to do."

"Doom," Hendrek remarked. "Then do you know the whole kingdom under the earth?"

"Virtually like no other," Snarks admitted. "As a truth-telling demon, it behooved me to move quickly and often through the Netherhells. In my formative youth, I therefore roamed the world underground from end to end. I would venture that I know as much about this place as any demon, for I have seen every nook and cranny along my kingdom's edge, and I have visited most of them. In a way, I feel it is fate that has brought us together, for in this quest, you could have no better guide than Snarks!"

His speech had been awfully reassuring. I just hoped

Snarks was telling the truth. And then I realized that he had to be.

The light was growing brighter and the tunnel wider as we continued our descent. I noticed as I turned to glance at my companions that the light gave Hendrek's complexion a greenish glow not too far different from Snarks's natural shade. I wondered, if we resided down below for great enough a time, if we would not all begin to resemble denizens of the Netherhells. It was not a pleasant thought to contemplate.

"I feel some trepidation," Snarks remarked. "It has been so long since I have seen my home. And yet will I be welcome there?" He sighed. "A demon without a country!"

We rounded another corner in the snaking tunnel. It was bright enough here to look for signs of some sort. A scrap of witch's clothing, perhaps, or a tumble of loose rocks where Norei had struggled with her captors. Might she have had time to etch some message into the dirt walls when the Dread Collectors paused to rest? But there was nothing beyond the constantly brightening rock about us.

"Are you sure they would have taken Norei this way?" I asked Snarks.

"No, the Dread Collectors would have taken her down some entirely different tunnel, then they'd come back and build this one just to fool us!" Snarks regarded me with demonic ire. "Sometimes I wonder about you humans! Of course they went this way! Quite some time ago by now. The Dread Collectors aren't too bright, but they're awfully fast. Don't worry. Even if we have to search the length and breadth of the Netherhells, we'll find her."

The demon pushed in front of me. "Oh, we're getting close now. I can already smell the sulfur!" Snarks emitted a high, raucous giggle.

"Doom!" Hendrek commented from the rear.

"My small green heart is palpitating!" Snarks cried as he ran ahead. "What part of the Netherhells will we see first? Maybe we are near the acid lakes. Then again, I think that Vushta was located above the East Netherhells Slime Pits!"

"Don't go too far!" I called to the rapidly advancing demon. "We don't want to get separated!" But Snarks was already out of sight.

"What is this?" his voice cried from some distance away. I thought I detected a note of panic.

"Doom!" Hendrek replied. The two of us rushed to help our comrade. We rounded one final corner and found Snarks at tunnel's end, staring out into a world of green light.

"Snarks!" I called. "Are you all right?"

The demon nodded dumbly.

Hendrek stepped to our compatriot's side, warclub at the ready. "Doom. Where are we, then? The acid lakes? The sulfur pools? The slime pits?"

"Oh, no!" Snarks whispered, gazing in horror at the vista before him. "I don't remember this at all!"

I looked out on truly the strangest sight I had ever seen. The scene before us was lit with signs that seemed to glow from within. They began at the tunnel mouth where we stood, and stretched in either direction for as far as the eye can see. Beneath each sign was a great window. Some windows were also lit from the inside, while others had great torches burning in front of their establishments. And the torches were also exceedingly strange, for they burned not only yellow and red, but blue and green as well.

Snarks swallowed grimly. "Well, you had best follow me anyway. There apparently have been some small changes in this neighborhood. I'm sure, once we start to walk, I'll recognize it immediately. We just have to move quickly and try not to attract attention."

We stepped from the tunnel mouth onto the green, glowing ground.

"Hey, you!" a voice called. "Yes, you! At the tunnel mouth! You looking for something?"

"Doom," Hendrek mumbled.

"Not necessarily," Snarks said. "Let me do the talking."

With some trepidation, Hendrek and I let the demon lead us away from the tunnel, our only means of escape. Snarks was walking straight for a short figure who waved at us in the distance. I told myself that we had to face up to the denizens of the Netherhells at some point. I had hoped, however, our first conversation would have been at a much later date.

"Hello!" Snarks called ahead. "Can you tell us exactly where we happen to be? I seem to be a bit lost."

The other demon hobbled in our direction. He appeared to be quite aged. "Little wonder, sonny," the old fellow wheezed. "Things have changed here a lot lately. You're out in the country now, halfway between the cities of Blecchh and Yurrghh."

"Between Blecchh and Yurrghh!" Snarks cried. "But that's unspoiled Netherhells countryside! Where is the brilliantly flowing magma? What happened to the pool of molten sulfur that I loved so much as a child?"

"Gone," the old fellow whined. "Covered over with what you see here, the Blecchh to Yurrghh Intercity Mall! Say, aren't those humans with you?"

"Yes, of course," Snarks said dismissively. "You mean the bramble fields are gone? And the poison berry groves? How could they do something like that?"

"It's called progress," the old demon replied. "Time was, you knew where you stood in the Netherhells. Now, if you stand too long in one place, they build a mall around you!"

"Doom." Hendrek looked darkly about him. "Then we are trapped in a—what was the word—mall?"

"So those are humans!" the old fellow exclaimed. "Say, sonny, just what are you folks doing here?"

"Oh, we are just here to rescue Vushta from the hands—"

Snarks yelped as I grabbed him and threw his hood over his face. "Mmmnffggllkfftt!"

It was only then that I realized the true nature of our peril. Snarks always had to tell the truth! If anyone were to ask him a direct question about our quest, he would answer it. And, should a demon in any authority ask, we were surely doomed.

"I am afraid what you ask is secret information!" I cried, trying to think fast. What would my master do in a situation like this? "We are here on a special human and demon cooperative mission, to—uh—deal with certain situations that affect both humans and demons!"

The old fellow smiled slyly. "So it does have something to do with that city they dragged through here a few days ago! Netherhells know where they're going to put it! Somebody mentioned they were going to stick it right smack in the middle of Upper Retch! Can you imagine what that will do to property values?"

"Doom," Hendrek said. "Upper Retch?"

Snarks tossed his hood away from his face. "The capital of all the Netherhells! Very interesting indeed!"

The old demon nodded. "It's been *real* interesting out here the past few days. Why, just a short while ago some Collectors ran on by here, toting a human female. Let me tell you, was that woman carrying on!"

"Oh, no! Was she screaming?" I asked before I could help myself.

"Nope." The old fellow shook his head. "Mostly she was yelling and beating the Collectors over the head with her fists. Let me tell you, she called those Collectors a few things we don't even say down in the Netherhells!"

I breathed a quiet sigh of relief. At least Norei was still alive, and she appeared to be as spirited as ever. Perhaps we could still rescue her before it was too late!

"Well, we had best be going," I said, anxious to be off.

"Doom," Hendrek added. "Nice meeting you."

"Demon and human relations, do you say?" the old fellow mused. "I think I might just come along."

Snarks frowned. "But you can't!"

"Oh?" The old fellow scratched his wrinkled green pate. "And why is that?"

"Oh," Snarks answered. "Because we have to go down and rescue mllffttgghhnnttrr!"

Once again, I had been forced to cover the demon's face with his hood. I realized I would have to say something as well to keep the old fellow from getting suspicious.

"This is dangerous work!" I insisted. "Of the greatest secrecy!"

"Oh, that's all right," the old-timer drawled. "I don't need to know all the fine points. Give me a moment to get my things. It really seems like a nice time to travel!"

"But this is your home!" I objected.

"Well, it was my home at one point, before it got 'revitalized.' That's what they say to you when they tear down your home to build a mall, you know. You're being 'revitalized'!"

Wouldn't this old fellow listen? "But we can't have too many people! We have to remain inconspicuous!"

The elder chuckled. "Two humans traveling with a demon who keeps hiding under a hood? I thought you were trying to draw attention to yourselves! I tell you what. If the demon here wants to take off his hood and give me one good reason not to come, I'll stay here in the mall."

We stood there for a moment in strained silence. At last, Snarks took off his hood.

"You'll have to bring something to eat," he advised. "All we have is human food."

"It's probably better than what they sell around here these days." The old fellow made a face. "The pies are full of artificial brambles!"

He bent over to reach behind a large circular container that bore the words DON'T BE A LITTER DEMON— HELP KEEP YOUR NETHERHELLS CLEAN! He pulled out a small sack and slung it over his shoulder.

"I'm as ready as I'll ever be," the elder said. "Who

knows? Maybe on our travels I can revitalize a thing or two myself!''

"Doom," Hendrek replied.

"That your name?" the oldster asked. "Has a nice ring to it. Folks call me Zzzzz."

"Doom," Hendrek repeated. "Zzzz?"

"No, no, Doom," the elder corrected. "Not four 'z's. Five. Zzzzz."

"Doom. My name is Hendrek."

"Hendrek?" Zzzzz scratched his wrinkled forehead. "Oh, so sorry. Doesn't have quite the same ring as Doom, though, does it?"

Hendrek opened his mouth to speak, but though better of it. Snarks and I each introduced ourselves.

"Well, now that we know each other," Zzzzz remarked, "what say we get started? I guess you've got a job to do."

I tried to make one final objection to the old demon accompanying us, but Snarks cut me off.

"No, Zzzzz is right in this," Snarks said. "Two demons and two humans is a much less conspicuous way to travel. After all, you could be our slaves."

"Slaves?" Hendrek commented. "Doom!"

"There's the word again!" Zzzzz interjected. "See how catchy that is? Maybe you should think about changing it."

"Whatever we do," Snarks insisted, "we must avoid detection."

So we began to walk down the long, green-glowing corridor, between two rows of buildings all too brightly lit. I heard faint music coming from somewhere.

A yellow demon clad in a loud orange-and-green-checked sportcoat sauntered out of a storefront before us. He waved an unlit cigar in our direction.

"Excuse me, gents," he said behind a smile that was far too wide. "Anybody got a light?"

It was Brax the Salesdemon.

# NINE

*Being trapped in the Netherhells is not the most fearsome thing that can happen to you. It is, in fact, probably no worse than being trapped in a cave for a weekend with all your spouse's relatives, and, in most cases, will not lead to total drooling, gibbering madness, as is the popular misconception. If, on the other hand, you find yourself trapped in the Netherhells for a weekend with all your spouse's relatives, well, sometimes drooling and gibbering can be fun.*

—*from* The Teachings of Ebenezum,
*Volume XXXIII*

"Doom!" Hendrek cried. He hoisted his warclub as I went for my sword. This foul demon would tell me what had happened to Norei!

Brax stepped back quickly. "Hendy baby! You and your friends misunderstand me completely! I am here to welcome you to the Netherhells!"

"You know these characters?" Zzzzz asked.

"I most certainly do!" Brax beamed. "One of them is a customer!"

"Oh, what a shame," Zzzzz frowned. "That must mean they're legitimate. It's really too bad. I had so much wanted to go and revitalize something before I died!"

"Well," Brax confided in a low tone, "they're not that legitimate!"

For some reason, Brax was not going to reveal our identities. What did this mean? And what had he done with Norei?

Snarks was gazing at the newcomer with barely controlled fury. "Fiend!" he shouted. "What have you and your kind done to my Netherhells?''

"I beg your pardon?" Brax replied mildly. "As far as I know, the Netherhells is right where it always was."

"That's beside the point!" Snarks insisted. "It's what has happened to the Netherhells. It's been—it's been . . ." Words seemed to fail him.

"Revitalized," Zzzzz suggested.

"Well, whatever!" Snarks continued. "What have you done to the countryside? Where are the acid lakes? Where are the sulfurous pools? Where are the slime pits?"

"Why," Brax said, a bit surprised, "they're still here. They've just been improved a bit."

"Improved?" Snarks challenged.

Brax waved his cigar aloft. "Surely. Just read the signs."

I looked up at the row of glowing signs that lined the top of the never-ending parade of buildings we had walked along. I hummed along with that quiet, ceaseless music as I read the placards. Brax was right. Directly before us was a place called "Acid City." A few doors beyond was another called "Sulfur Universe." And we stood before a door marked "Slime-O-Rama, Home of the Famous Slime Burger!"

"It's no use!" Snarks wailed. "Your kind will never understand!"

"Maybe we can revitalize him!" Zzzzz suggested hopefully.

"Hold it, hold it!" Brax snapped two fingers together to produce a flame. He puffed his cigar alight. "As I said before, you guys have got me all wrong. Believe it or not, I'm on your side."

"Doom!" Hendrek lifted Headbasher aloft.

"Hear me out! Hear me out!" The salesdemon danced away. "After all, now you're in my neck of the woods."

I placed my hand on the warrior's shoulder. "He's right, Hendrek. We should listen to him. After he tells us what he has done with Norei!"

"At last. Someone with some common sense." Brax smiled in my direction. "Maybe I could sell you a good used weapon some day. But that's not the reason I'm here. At least not directly."

"Does it have to do with Norei?" I demanded. "Where is she?"

Brax blew a smoke ring in my direction. "The Collectors have taken her. Just as well. I never knew a human could be so much trouble. Not even Hendrek!"

"Doom!"

"But that's my whole point!" The demon jabbed his cigar toward Hendrek for emphasis. "Humans were meant to give demons problems, as demons were meant to bedevil humanity. Guxx Unfufadoo is a big thinker, perhaps too big. He wants to take over the surface world and run everything! But, if demons control both above and below ground, who do I have left to sell used weapons to? It's that simple, gentlebeings. If the Netherhells take over the surface world, I'm out of a job!"

"Take over the surface?" Zzzzz marveled. "This is bigger than I thought! Oh, there's going to be some revitalization for sure!"

"Perhaps you have a point, friend Snarks," Brax continued. "We have made all the progress we see around us, but is demonkind happy? Why do the Netherhells want to take over the surface, anyway? It's negative feelings about their own kingdom, that's why! I say, rather than disrupt the order of things, let's develop a more positive image of our own home caves! Up with the Netherhells!"

Brax paused as if he expected the rest of us to echo the cheer.

"Doom," Hendrek said to fill the silence.

"Indeed," I added a moment later. I had to be careful. The logic of a fiend like Brax could be very slippery. "You say you are against the Netherhells taking over the surface world. Then why did you assist Guxx by abducting Norei?"

"Oh, I knew that would come up!" Cigar smoke

wafted from Brax's nostrils as he sighed. "Yes, I was working for Guxx there, wasn't I? Well, there were two reasons. The first is you do not say no to Guxx Unfufadoo. You may have noticed that as well. The slightest misstep and he throws one of his rhymes at you!" The demon shivered.

"But it was working for Guxx that made me decide on this course of action. I realized that if he got what he wanted, all of humankind and all of demonkind would be changed forever!"

"Indeed," I replied. "And how can we believe you?"

"Not believe honest Brax?" The demon blew another smoke ring. "I have already made a gesture of good faith. I only took the young witch, Norei. I had been sent to capture the wizard Ebenezum!"

The demon did have a point. I paused a moment to consider.

"But why are we all so glum?" Brax continued. "Now, now, you just haven't gotten into the spirit of this yet! The underworld can still be a fun place. If you listen carefully, and the wind is right, you can still sometimes hear the screams of the damned! The Netherhells forever!"

"Now wait a minute," Snarks interjected. "I was the one who was nostalgic for the Netherhells countryside —the magma, the brambles, the slime pools. I was banished to the surface world! You don't know how much I longed to come back!"

"Exactly! That's the attitude I want to see! More loyalty to the Netherhells' grand traditions! In fact, I've come up with a whole series of jingles and clever sayings for that very purpose. Listen to this." Brax cleared his throat and sang in a gravelly tenor.

> If we don't have it, it can't be got!
> The Netherhells is hot, hot, hot!

"I don't think I want to come back anymore," Snarks muttered.

Well, no matter what Snarks said, it was sort of catchy. "Indeed," I remarked in my best wizard tone. "And what do you want from us?"

"Why, to work side by side." Brax opened his arms to include us all. "The Netherhells should be for demonkind! I think we should put Vushta back where it belongs!"

I frowned at Brax. If we were to work together, we would have to strike a bargain. "Will you help us to find Norei?"

"And have her hit me over the head again?" The demon sighed. "Very well. If I must."

I looked to Snarks and Hendrek. "What do you think?"

"Doom," Hendrek replied.

"We need to speak alone," was Snarks's answer.

The truth-telling demon and I moved a few stores away from the others. Snarks spoke to me in a low voice.

"Trust me," Snarks said. "You never want to trust a demon."

"Indeed," I replied. "Still, he knows of our whereabouts, and he knows of our purpose. Isn't it better that we keep him with us, rather than rejecting him and not knowing what he is up to?"

"You have a point!" Snarks admitted. "I tell you. What you can learn about people in times of peril! You were always good with that staff of yours. I never knew you could think, too!"

"Indeed," I agreed. "Still, I wish there was some way I could have my master's counsel in this."

Snarks slapped me on the back. "But there is a way to talk to your master! That's why he gave you a magic sword!" The demon shook his head. "Isn't that just like a human! Do I have to tell you everything?"

Of course! Ebenezum had told me that we could communicate through the sword! There was no time to lose! I pulled Cuthbert swiftly from its scabbard.

"What do you want?" the sword shrieked.

"We must use your magic to talk with my master," I replied.

"Oh, thank goodness," the sword said in a relieved tone. "I thought you expected me to kill someone or something! It's all this dried ichor on me. It's very disorienting!"

Perhaps the sword was right. I untucked my shirt and did my best to rub the ichor off.

"Ah, that brightens my outlook on life, let me tell you!" the sword remarked. "Remember, a clean sword is a happy sword! Now, who is it that you want to contact?"

"You must contact Ebenezum!" I insisted.

"Who?" the sword queried.

"Ebenezum, " Snarks interjected. "He's a wizard back in East Vushta. Is there anything else you need to know? Perhaps we should contact Ebenezum ourselves and bring him to you!"

"Please!" Cuthbert cried, deeply offended. "We swords may look like simple tools of power and mayhem, but we harbor sensitive souls within." The weapon paused for a moment, as if gathering its reserves. "You. The fellow who is holding me. What is your name?"

"W-wuntvor," I stammered in surprise.

"Wuntvor!" Cuthbert repeated with satisfaction. "Very pleased to meet you. No one ever thinks to introduce anybody to a magic sword. It's just pull you out, hack, slice, hack, and back in the scabbard again. I mean, what's the use of being magic?"

"Indeed," I replied. "So could we contact Ebenezum now?"

"Oh, certainly," the sword responded. "It's so difficult being stuck in the scabbard all day. I mean, if you can never talk about it, what's the use of being magic? Oh, the contact! Now, lift me over your head and swing me around three times. I'll do the rest!"

I did as the sword instructed. The first time I swung the sword, a small light appeared before me. The second swing, and the light grew to the size of an apple. On the third swing, the light exploded outward, until it appeared we were looking through a window right onto the lawn at the Academy of Magic and Sorcery Extension Program campus!

"Your wizardship!" Klothus called across the greensward. "I have your robes for you at last!"

"Indeed?" came a voice from outside the picture. "Bring them here quickly! There is work to be done."

Klothus moved across the lawn. The image in the window blurred and shifted. When it cleared again, Klothus stood before my master!

"Here they are," the costumer said with some pride. "Just as you specified, model four-seventeen!"

And yes, they were just what my master ordered. The magical window was clear enough so even I could see the delicately embroidered silver moons and stars.

"Excellent!" Ebenezum cried. "Now I can once again truly feel the part of the wizard!" He eagerly unfolded the robes that Klothus had given him. But then he paused and frowned, lifting a short piece of cloth that was sewn to the main body of the garment.

"Indeed," my master inquired. "And what is this?"

"Oh?" Klothus replied dismissively. "What else would that be? It's a short sleeve."

"Short sleeves?" My master's voice trembled. I could see his anger grow as he rapidly unfolded the rest of the garment.

"Well," Klothus said rapidly as he sensed my master's growing displeasure, "I told you the resources of the college here are somewhat limited. That robe is a four-seventeen. It's the summer model. I did not think you would mind. While it is no longer high summer, it is still somewhat warm. Well, at least warmish . . ."

Klothus's voice died as Ebenezum stared at him, the robes held at arm's length from the wizard's body. From the look on my master's face, you could tell he was not pleased.

Klothus seemed to evaporate from the window. I guessed he had made a silent retreat. Looking at the costume he held, I could see Ebenezum's point. In an emergency, perhaps, my master might have been capable of wearing the upper part of the modified summer tunic, but I could never have seen him wearing the shorts.

"It's probably none of my business," Cuthbert remarked from above my head, "but now that I've gone to all the trouble of making magical contact, don't you think you should say something?"

The sword was right! I had come upon this quest half certain that I would never see the surface world again. I had been so overwhelmed to see my master once more, in obviously good spirits, that I had temporarily forgotten my purpose!

But what should I say?

I cleared my throat.

"Excuse me?" I began.

My master started violently. He turned to look into the magic window.

"Indeed!" he cried. "Wuntvor!"

"Indeed!" I replied. "Master!"

"So that sword is working after all!" Ebenezum tugged reflectively at his beard. "Frankly, Wunt, after seeing the condition of this place's underground storage vaults, I had my doubts."

"Not that it's any of my business," Cuthbert interjected, "but don't you think you should ask him your question? I mean, I can't keep up this magic window business all day!"

The sword was right again. Quickly, I filled my master in with regards to Brax.

"I believe," my master said when I was done, "your decision was the best for the moment, Wunt. Still, I am glad you called me. This way, in case Brax is involved in some secondary Netherhells scheme, we will be ready for it. There's no way they can surprise us now."

I smiled at that. I, too, was glad I called my master! But was there anything else I should discuss with him while we still maintained magical contact?

"Excuse us, Ebenezum," a deep voice said from somewhere. Hubert stuck his dragon head into the magic picture. "If we might just have a moment—why, look who's out there! Alea!"

Alea's blond curls danced brilliantly into the frame. "Wuntie! How good to see you! We've been working on that heroic song about you, Wuntie, ever since you left! I think we're really getting it nearly right now, something that combines your vulnerability with a real sense of danger."

"Yeah!" Hubert added. "It's bound to be a hit!"

Alea and Hubert glanced at each other for the merest of moments.

"Look, Wuntvor," Alea began. "We know you don't have much time—"

"Yeah!" Hubert interrupted. "But maybe if we sing a couple bars, it'll spur you on your way! Hit it, damsel!"

> Wuntvor was a youth who had nothing to hide
> Went on a mission that was suicide—

The picture vanished.

"I'm sorry." There was a note of condescension in Cuthbert's tone. "I don't use my magic window for projecting vaudeville!"

"Indeed," I replied. I lowered the sword and turned it about to slide it back into its sheath.

"Must we be so hasty!?" Cuthbert blurted. "Magic swords can be a lot of fun, you know. Can't I stay out just a little while longer and ta—"

Sword back in place, I nodded to Snarks. I had spoken with Ebenezum. It was time to continue our quest.

"Well," Brax said when we rejoined the salesdemon, "what are we waiting for?"

"Revitalization, here we come!" Zzzzz cheered.

"Doom," Hendrek added as he took up the rear.

On we walked, down the never-ending row of brightly lit establishments, any one of which would put the gaudiest inn on the surface world to shame. I had been afraid to look within these strange structures, fearful that I might be enticed inside by some Netherhells trick. But now that we walked mere feet away from the gaudily painted windows and doors, some even surrounded by multicolored torches, I found my eyes wandering repeatedly toward whatever might lay inside. Smiling demons waved as we passed, holding aloft arcane and complicated contraptions that I was happy I did not yet know the use for.

I hummed along with the ever-present, faint music. Actually, it seemed louder here. Wait a moment. Why was I walking so quickly by these charming storefronts? I thought again on the contraption I had seen the demon show me one window back. Actually, that thing had been rather novel, in its way. Now that I thought of it, I really had to go back to that window and look at it once again! Yes! It was the very thing I needed! I would go in there and get it right now. Wait! I didn't have any money! On, no matter. I was sure they would take a magic sword in barter. I could not live without it! There was the perfect place for it in my den.

"Hendrek!" I heard Snarks cry. "Grab him quickly!"

"Doom!" The large warrior wrapped his arms around me and pulled me away from the door.

"But I have to!" I shouted. "I need it for my den!"

Hendrek shook me roughly. What was I saying? I must have been under some sort of spell. I didn't even have a den. I didn't even know what a den was!

Snarks confirmed my suspicion. "Netherhells Buying Fever," he said grimly. "Lucky we got you before it was too late. Once you begin to shop . . ." The demon shivered.

Somewhat shakily, I resumed the march. At Snarks's suggestion, we moved more quickly than before.

Brax sidled up to me as we walked. "By the way," he remarked, his voice barely above a whisper, "I've been meaning to talk to you."

"Indeed?" I responded. I would have to do my best not to let Brax see how shaken I still was. Maybe now I could learn the demon's true purpose.

"Well, I tell you," he continued, "I couldn't help but notice that you have a magic sword."

A chill went down my spine. What was he getting at?

"Indeed?" I said after a moment. "What do you mean?"

"Oh, don't act coy with me. I have an eye for this sort of thing. It's something you develop in the used-weapon business."

Brax paused dramatically before he spoke again.

"Listen. Do you know how much money there is in magic swords?"

I told Brax that I did not.

"I didn't think so. You may be sitting on a gold mine there!" The demon smiled convivially. "Or at least you have one hitched to your belt!"

"Indeed?" That was it! Only moments ago, the deadly sales forces of the Netherhells almost had me in their grasp. Now this demon wanted to take my only weapon and leave me defenseless! But I had discerned his insidious plan. Somehow I would have to outsmart this foul fiend!

"I could offer you a pretty price for it," Brax added when it became clear that I would say no more.

"Indeed," I said reflectively.

"That's all?" Brax complained. "Just 'indeed'? Here I am, offering you riches untold for one measly little sword and you won't even give me a simple yes or no? Ah, say no more, human. You are a shrewd bargainer. I can foresee a whole new career for you." The demon's voice lowered to a more confidential tone. "Listen, after this is all over, I was thinking about setting up some franchise operations above ground. You might be exactly the sort of fellow—"

"Doom!" The bold Hendrek interrupted the sales-demon's spiel.

I looked up to see what had caused the large warrior's outburst. A whole section of the Netherhells mall seemed to have been totally destroyed. After seeing nothing but one establishment after another with names like "Pitchfork Paradise" and "Lost Soul City," we had come to a stretch where there was nothing but debris.

"Revitalization," Zzzzz whispered in wonder.

"I think not," Snarks replied grimly. He picked up a sign that read MAX'S BLASTER FURNACE! and then in smaller letters below: *Hot enough for you? It will be inside!*

"This does not seem to fit in with the Netherhells idea of progress," Snarks continued. "I smell human intervention here. This is part of the counterattack!"

So Ebenezum and the other wizards were already making themselves known! I stepped carefully through torn bits of wood and broken glass. The carnage here certainly was impressive. Perhaps we could defeat the Netherhells after all!

"Doom," Hendrek repeated.

And he was right. I felt it, too. It was odd, in a way, how quickly one became used to the nature of something. We had been walking through this strange mall for mere moments, yet I had already grown used to the never-ending rows of strangely named buildings with their bright displays and demonically smiling shopkeepers. While I knew that with every step through the Netherhells we were in danger, somehow that parade of shops had made it a controllable danger.

Now, though, we had stepped into chaos. Debris was scattered everywhere, pieces of displays, parts of goods, decimated building materials, perhaps even pieces of demons. The detritus covered virtually every inch of the green glowing ground, plunging the whole region into a darkness far more profound than any I had ever seen on the surface.

"Mmmmmmm!" came the cry from my belt.

Of course! I drew forth Cuthbert, the enchanted sword.

"That's more like it," the sword sighed as it burst into light. "I don't have to kill anybody, do I?"

"No, no," I quickly reassured the sword. "It just got a little dark down here."

"And you need a little light?" Cuthbert chortled. "That's the kind of job I was made for!"

We walked in silence for a moment.

"Why do you think it's so dark?" the sword added with some trepidation.

"Indeed," I mused. "There are signs here of a recent battle." I kicked the remains of a placard out of my path. The battle seemed to have been of some proportion. Had Ebenezum and his fellows at the college conjured up a magical army to come to our aid?

"Battle?" the sword shrilled. "Oh, I knew this whole thing would come to no good. Perhaps you should place me back in my scabbard. I mean, do you need me around that desperately? It isn't that dark now, is it?"

Actually the sword was right. It was getting lighter as we walked. We seemed to be reaching the end of whatever great struggle had taken place. In the distance, I could see where the row of stores resumed, all of them still brightly lit.

Brax was at my side again. "You've been holding out on me! You didn't tell me that the sword could talk!"

"Indeed," I replied, intent on looking ahead to where the stores resumed. "You did not ask!"

Was it my imagination, or did I hear the faint sound of battle?

"Wait a moment!" Cuthbert cried. "Do I hear someone appreciating me? Yes, I certainly do talk! And how about this light!" The sword glowed even more fiercely.

"Actually, glowing magic swords are fairly common," Brax remarked. "Intelligent conversation, on the other hand, is much more unusual."

"Conversation, perhaps," Snarks put in. "I don't think anyone here ever mentioned the word intelligent."

"You," Cuthbert whined. "Are you the one who called me *measly*?"

Snarks threw his hands forward protectively. "No, I would never say anything like that. I, for one, know your true worth." He pointed at Brax. "It was the other demon!"

"The other demon?" Cuthbert shrieked. "You mean the one admiring me? You two-faced denizen of the Netherhells! You play with fire when you toy with a magic sword!"

"Who, me?" Brax smiled endearingly behind his cigar. "I am but a poor salesdemon, trying to eke out a living. What did I say?"

"I heard you distinctly. You referred to me as 'one measly little sword'! I know! That's what people think of you when all you can do is hack and slash! I tell you, I wouldn't have this problem if I were a magic mirror!"

"Doom," said Hendrek close to my ear. "I thought that the sword could not hear when it was placed inside the scabbard."

Hendrek was right. I had been under the same impression. I pulled the sword down in front of my eyes and inquired as to the discrepancy.

"Oh. Only a little white lie," Cuthbert admitted. "You don't know how boring owners can be. Whenever they pull me out, they always go on and on about honor and valor and stuff like that. Ah, but when they put me away, it's a different matter! I tell you, I hear some of the best bits when I'm not supposed to be able to hear at all!"

For my part, I heard a great crash before us. We had come quite close to the other end of the debris-laden no-demon's-land. In fact, that crash had come from the mall.

"Doom," Hendrek said.

I thought about returning Cuthbert to his scabbard to put an end to his arguing. But I might have quick need of a sword, and anyone standing within a mile or so of our present location had surely heard us by now. Still, perhaps whatever small army was fighting within would be too busy to bother with us and let us continue on our way.

The mall road curved ahead so we could not see more than a half dozen buildings before us. We did, however, hear the three voices call in unison from somewhere far ahead.

"We will catch the intruders."

"Doom!" Hendrek voiced what I thought. " 'Tis the Dread Collectors!"

"We will throw them in prison!" the voices, now closer, cried as one.

Another loud crash came from the shop to our left. Perhaps we could hide in one of the buildings! But the storefronts here were dark and the doors bolted against catastrophe.

"We will trap them there forever!" the voices, now quite distinct, chanted in unison.

"Quick!" Snarks urged. "We have to do something!"

A foot flew through the window of the building to our left, right through the painted sign that read "Snurff's House of Degradation." The foot withdrew within the building, followed by a chorus of screams.

# TEN

*Magic weapons can, on occasion, be of great use, yet one more part of the truly rounded wizard's arsenal of tricks, spells, and remarks for all occasions. However, the thoroughly prepared mage will find certain spells of even more importance than these, especially those enchantments which produce magic wings, magic carpets, and magic running boots, for those times when the rest of your arsenal fails you completely.*

—*from* The Teachings of Ebenezum,
*Volume LVII*

As bad as it sounded outside of Snurff's House of Degradation, it was much worse inside. Whatever the original purpose of the shop had been, it now looked like its sole purpose was to sell debris. The air was full of dust and the ground crunched and snapped beneath our feet. I drew Cuthbert again from its midnight-blue scabbard, but even the sword's magic light was lost in this gloom. I instructed Snarks to grab hold of my belt, and Hendrek to grasp Snarks's hood, and so on down the line. With the atmosphere this murky, the only way we might stay together was to form a living chain.

"Do I have to be out here?" Cuthbert whined. "I warn you, I tarnish very easily!"

I told the sword to be still. There were other voices up ahead.

"You!" a particularly nasty voice screamed. "You really disgust me!"

"Glurph!" a second, equally nasty voice cried in panic. "I don't think he came here for that!"

"Remember the really bad things your mother used to call you when she was mad at you?" the first nasty voice continued. "Well, she was right! Except she was your mother, so she was being too kind!"

"Glurph!" the second voice screamed. "You'll only make him angrier!"

"You remember when you failed that examination? When you forgot your beloved's birthday? You thought you were unworthy! You called yourself a miserable worm, unfit to do anything but crawl through the earth on your belly! Well, *you* were being too kind! Even the ground under your feet is too good—"

"Glurph! Are you crazy? You keep this up and we're both dead demons!"

"No!" the first nasty voice shouted in triumph. "I know precisely what I'm saying to this miserable piece of slime! I was born a degrader. I lived as a degrader. Now let me die as a degrader! Urrracchhtt!"

There was a thump, as if something heavy had fallen to the floor.

"Glurph?" the other voice said tentatively. "Oh, I see. Look, I can be much more pleasant than that dead fellow over there. Really! For example, I'm sure your mother didn't really mean all those terrible things she said about you. Oh, surely, there must have been some truth in—urracchhtt!"

There was another heavy thump and a large, black-clothed, extremely well muscled shape loomed before me.

"Not satisfying," the shape said. "Not satisfying at all."

With a sudden shock, I realized that I recognized that shape and the voice behind it.

"You!" I exclaimed.

The shape turned around, a man dressed all in black, a symphony of perfectly tuned muscles in motion.

"Oh, excuse me," a mild voice said. "I haven't seen you in quite some time."

I was right! It was the Dealer of Death!

I held Cuthbert before me. "Come!" I shouted. "Try to take me, if you must!"

"Wait a second!" the sword cried. "What are you doing!? Is this a fight? Don't I get to say anything about this?"

"A talking sword?" The Dealer's well muscled face smiled. "Now that is interesting. Very little has been of any interest whatsoever, you know, since my descent into the Netherhells!"

"That's right, I'm a talking sword! And I really want to ask you two fellows to talk things over! It's amazing how often bloodshed may be avoided with a little reasoned discussion—"

"I beg your pardon?" the Dealer inquired. "Who said anything about bloodshed?"

"Oh, well," Cuthbert coughed. "I just assumed, being a drawn sword and all—"

"On the contrary, Wuntvor and I here—I did recall your name right, did I not?—anyway, Wuntvor and I have nothing at all to fight about. Oh, it is true that I had a contract to kill him and his two companions, one Ebenezum and one Hendrek, I believe, but that was back on the surface world. Besides, as you may recall, the king who gave me the contract was being a little stingy and perhaps more than a little underhanded in his terms. I've had a lot of time to think since I've come to the Netherhells, and I've come up with a great many questions about that particular contract's legality. Therefore, if I'm going to kill Wuntvor, I can't do so until after I renegotiate the contract in question." The Dealer smiled with muscular lips. "So there's nothing to fight about whatsoever!"

"Thank goodness!" Cuthbert cried. "See what a little talking can do?"

"Excuse me," I said to the Dealer as I pointed the sword toward its scabbard.

"Where are you putting me?" Cuthbert complained. "I was getting interested! You can't—"

"There," I said with some satisfaction. The scabbard allowed us to hear only the most muted of overwrought mumblings. "Indeed," I said to the Dealer. "I believe you had your hand in all the destruction we saw on our way here?"

The Dealer smiled again. "In all humility, I must say I did have something to do with it." He flexed his great muscles absently. "It all has to do with frustration, really. I've strangled thousands of demons. I'm afraid the fun's going out of it. Ah, sometimes I long for the simple pleasures of the surface world. I say, one of you wouldn't happen to have a wild pig handy?"

A quick conference revealed that no one had stashed a pig.

"A pity." The Dealer tried to smile through his disappointment. "Oh, well, it was an insane hope. I so enjoy strangling pigs. It's a real hands-on experience! You can't get that kind of grip on a demon, you know." The Dealer made a particularly muscular frown. "Demons tend to squish."

"Indeed," I replied, sensing that it was time to change the subject. "We are on our way to rescue Vushta. Would you like to come along?"

"Rescue Vushta?" the Dealer asked. "Where has it gotten itself to?"

I explained briefly about the dastardly attack of the Netherhells.

"Oh, that does sound rather more interesting than what I've been doing of late." The Dealer cracked his large and impressive knuckles. "I'll still be squishing demons, I suppose, but now I'll be doing it for a cause! You don't suppose there'd be a wild pig or two left in Vushta, do you?"

"Anything is possible," I suggested.

"One can still dream." The Dealer sighed wistfully. His breath cleared the dust from half the room. "But there are more demons here!"

I hastily explained that Snarks, Brax, and Zzzzz had joined us on our quest.

"It is a strange land here, with strange customs." The muscles in the Dealer's neck rippled as he nodded his head. "I will abide by your guidance. My skills have become dulled down here. I think rescuing the largest city in the known world from hordes of demonic fiends is exactly the sort of thing I need to hone my reflexes. It sounds like it will be extremely difficult and very, very bloody!'' The Dealer laughed with delight at the thought.

"Good," I replied. "Then we should be on our way. Is there a back way out of here?"

Before the Dealer could respond, I heard three other voices cry as one: "We have found you!"

"Doom!" Hendrek moaned, Headbasher at the ready.

The shapes moved toward us through the dust-laden store.

"The Dread Collectors!" cried Snarks.

"Revitalization at last!" cried Zzzzz.

"Hey, fellows?" cried Brax. "We used to work together! Remember me?"

"Collectors?" the Dealer inquired. "Perhaps they have stronger necks than demons! Perhaps it will feel much like strangling a wild pig!"

"We have come to take you prisoner," the three voices proclaimed as one. And then the claws and teeth came for us.

Hendrek's warclub somehow deflected one tearing, howling mass of death. I pulled Cuthbert free of its sheath.

"What?" the sword screamed. "What are you doing now? Let's run away! I don't want to get involved in this again!"

"It will be easier if you do not resist us!" the three voices exhorted as they slashed and bit.

Brax danced away from the triple engine of mayhem, waving his cigar. Snarks and Zzzzz rooted through the debris of the shop for something they might use as a weapon.

"We do not plan to kill you yet!" the three horrible voices chanted.

Snarks came up with some sort of long metal bar,

which he expertly twirled around to keep a Collector's claws at bay. Zzzzz threw bits of broken glass and pottery as he shouted "Revitalization! Revitalization!" in a high and eerie tone.

"We must deliver you to the demon Guxx Unfufadoo!" the Collectors all cried. "Before you die, Guxx must torture the truth from you!"

I felt a sudden moment of fear. What if that was what the Collectors had done with Norei? Had my beloved perished some horrible way at the hands of that foul fiend, Guxx Unfufadoo? If so, then all the Netherhells would pay!

"Easy there!" Cuthbert screamed as I slashed at the nearest Collector. "Watch out! Coming through!"

My sword grazed the thing's dark and oily pelt. Green ichor once again stained the blade.

"Now see what you've made me do?" Cuthbert squealed, absolutely beside itself. "Oh, I can't tell you how much I hate ichor!"

I barely dodged a set of raging Collector's claws as I watched the Dealer launch himself onto the thing's back.

"Where's the neck?" the Dealer bellowed as he felt rapidly beneath the thing's pelt. "Hold still for a moment so I can find your neck!"

"Doom!" Hendrek cried as he smashed Headbasher into a Collector whose claws were perilously close to my head.

"We can defeat these things!" the large warrior called to me. "Let us stand back to back. I will have at the fiends with my club while you stab away with your sword!"

"Must we?" Cuthbert wailed.

And then I realized that I did not have to wield my sword! The last time, I had defeated these foul things through the use of another of my magical weapons —Wonk, the horn of persuasion! But Wonk was in a sack which I had set aside when I began the fight. Where had I put it?

"Look out!" Cuthbert screamed in a voice much higher than usual. I was looking straight down a black hole bordered all around with sharp Collector fangs!

Blue sparks flew as Cuthbert bounced off the thing's razor teeth. I leaped sideways. The jaws snapped shut inches from my face. And the thing kept on going, toward the back of the large warrior who was fighting behind me!

"Hendrek!" I cried as the slavering creature descended upon him, jaws open so wide that it made the huge warrior seem no more than a child.

"Doom!" Hendrek's voice echoed in the vast cavern of the Collector's mouth as the warrior spun about to face it. His warclub came down full force upon the foul thing's nose.

The Collector staggered back.

"Urk!" all three Collectors howled as one.

"Doom!" the large warrior intoned. He swung his warclub in ever-widening arcs above his head. "We have them now! Doom! Doom! Doom!"

Snarks appeared at Hendrek's side, twirling his iron pipe. Zzzzz had found a long jagged plank, which he wielded much as I used to handle my stout oak staff. He stepped to Hendrek's other side. The Dealer still rode one of the Collectors somewhere out in the vast dust-filled shop, crying, "The neck! Where's the neck?"

We did seem to have the upper hand. But it was all too easy. Where was the third Collector?

My eyes swept that part of the room I could see through the dust, searching for the third fearsome monster. It had seemed too easy to defeat the fiends this time. Were the three Collectors luring us into some sort of trap?

And then my gaze fell on the sack that contained Wonk, the horn of persuasion. If I could reach that fearsome instrument and blow but a single note, whatever trap the Collectors were planning would evaporate as fast as the quick-moving fiends could disappear.

"Listen." Brax's voice came from somewhere.

"There must be some way we can compromise!"

I moved, rapidly but carefully, toward the sack. Brax ran from the dust-laden darkness, his lit cigar like a beacon before him.

"Well, you can't say I didn't try—oof!" he grunted as he ran into my quickly moving legs.

I yelled as I fell. My sword yelled as it was flung from my grasp.

I felt a weight upon my back. A sharp point pricked at my skin. I feared it was a Collector's claw.

I could still see Hendrek from where I lay. He swung once again for the Collector's nose. But this time the thing's claws, moving even faster than the warrior's enchanted weapon, lifted both club and man aloft. The Collector casually tossed Hendrek over its shoulder.

"Dooooooo—" And then his voice was lost in the dust and the distance. The Dealer was similarly tossed away, as a horse might remove a fly.

"We will take you to Guxx now," three voices said in unison. The claw at my back grasped my shirt and lifted me aloft.

"Wait a minute!" Snarks protested as a Collector bent to pick him up. "I'm a demon!"

"So we noticed." The Collector who held me shook me in Snarks's direction. "Is this then a demon in disguise?"

"No," Snarks admitted. "Actually, that's a young wizard intent on rescuing Vushta from the clutches of the Netherhells."

"So we thought," the Collectors intoned. "We will take him to be tortured by Guxx."

The three Collectors turned and marched from the store, one by one. The one that carried me moved after the other two. It slung me over its shoulder. I stared in horror at Snarks, rapidly shrinking in the distance.

Snarks shrugged. "I cannot tell a lie."

# ELEVEN

*"What?" you cry. "Wizards sometimes must endure torture?" And it is true, for being a wizard does not exempt you from any of the trials and tribulations experienced by other humans.*

*But I would ask you to consider just what you mean by "torture." What of those occasions when you save a kingdom and then are forced to sit there and listen for hours to endless numbers of boring elected officials extolling your praises while the kingdom's tax collectors repossess nine-tenths of what you gainfully earned at your task? Is this not torture? What about the times when you are on the verge of creating a spell that will give you inner peace at last and your spouse bursts into your study and tells you to clean up the mess because all of your in-laws are coming to stay for three weeks, and we will have to set up a bed in here because Aunt Sadie needs a place to sleep? Is this not torture? And say you are attending a wizard's convention and are sure that your gold production spell will win first prize in the competition, and then they give the award to the animal husbandry spell of some part-time wizard because the judge has a particular fondness for pigs? Is this not—but why belabor the obvious? By now you surely see my point. Laugh in the face of torture! It is, after all, no worse than what they do to you every other day of the week.*

—*from* Ask Ebenezum: The Greatest Wizard in the
Western Kingdoms Answers the Four Hundred
Most Asked Questions about Wizardry,
*fourth edition*

So now I would be tortured by Guxx. I would perish in some horribly complicated, painful way, far from my homeland, having failed both my master and the entire surface world. I tried to think of some positive aspect of my situation. So far, I could not come up with one.

"We will take you to the dungeon," all three Collectors said.

"Indeed!" I cried, eager to keep these creatures talking. Perhaps I could get them to reveal some secret of the Netherhells that I could somehow use to my advantage. "Will I meet Guxx there?"

"We will leave you at the dungeon until Guxx is ready!" the three monstrosities answered. "He will torture you at his leisure!"

So Guxx wouldn't get me immediately! In an odd way, it was almost heartening. I would find some way yet to escape from these fiends and continue with my quest! They had not heard the last from Wuntvor the apprentice!

"Indeed," I continued. "And what will you do?"

"We?" the Collectors chorused. "We must collect!"

These creatures were still not telling me anything I did not already know. I would have to question them more closely.

"And do you always take what you collect to the dungeons?" I asked tentatively.

"No, we do not!" The Collectors turned as one, moving down a passageway that cut away at right angles from the constant row of stores.

My heart leaped. I remembered, long ago, my master telling me about magical creatures sometimes having hidden weaknesses. Perhaps there was some secret code or special bit of magic that would force these demonic monsters to free me!

"Indeed!" I remarked. Perhaps, if I was clever, I could discover the weakness that would allow me to escape from the Collectors before I ever saw the dungeon!

"And what happens to those you do not take to jail?" I asked craftily.

"Oh!" the creatures replied calmly. "We rip them into tiny shreds!"

"Indeed," I replied with somewhat less enthusiasm. Then again, perhaps this was not the proper line of questioning after all. What should I try next? Perhaps I should quiz them on their home lives.

"We are here!" The Collectors stated proudly.

"Here?" I said. "Where?"

I was unceremoniously dropped in the dirt.

"Your home," the Collectors added, "for the rest of your life!"

I looked up beyond the three fanged horrors. There before me was a great wall of greenish gray, topped with a row of daggers. Beyond the daggers stood a dozen blood-red hounds who snarled down at whatever had the misfortune to lurk on the wall's other side. Directly before me was a gate that seemed somehow to be composed completely of sharpened spikes. Above the gate was a great sign, carved in stone ten feet high:

NETHERHELLS MOST HORRENDOUS
DUNGEON NUMBER FOUR
JUNIOR DIVISION

And below that, in words two feet high:

LOSE VIRTUALLY ALL HOPE YE WHO ENTER HERE

"For the rest of my life?" I whispered.

The gate of spikes opened seemingly of its own accord and the fattest demon I had ever seen waddled forth. Bright purple in color, he reminded me of nothing so much as a grape with legs.

"Don't worry," the bloated demon remarked. "Your life won't be all that long." The fiend waved at the Collectors. "You have done your job well. The doomed soul is mine now. You may go."

"We go to collect!" The three massive monsters turned in unison and ambled back up the passageway.

"I am called Urrpphh!" The bloated demon grinned fiendishly. "And I am your master, at least for what little time you have left!" Urrpphh laughed hideously, as if he had said something funny.

"But I must introduce you to my minions," the demon continued. "Come to me, my lovelies!"

"Slobber!" they cried as they poured from the gates. "Slobber! Slobber!"

I knew what they were in an instant. I had seen trolls before; tall, dark, muscular, but mostly mouth, rather like a walking set of very sharp teeth.

One of them tentatively put its mouth around my head.

"No! No!" Urrpphh shouted. "Not to eat! To torture!"

"No slobber?" the troll whined, genuinely disappointed.

"Come," the demon said graciously. "Allow my minions and me to escort you around the grounds."

We entered a large enclosure full of the green glowing moss I had seen elsewhere in my travels underground. It almost looked like an open field. It might even have been pleasant were it not for the screams I heard in the distance.

"Oh, those?" Urrpphh said as I winced. "Yes, you will become more familiar with those as time progresses."

Urrpphh and his trolls led me to the first of a series of low buildings built in a circle around the edge of the field. A heavily spiked door swung open as we approached.

"My office." Urrpphh waved me in before him. "You are welcome to visit at any time. Number Four, you see, is a merciful dungeon. When your torture has become truly unbearable, you may come here to grovel on your hands and knees, perhaps even on your belly, and beg for mercy. Not, of course, that it will do any good."

I looked about the virtually featureless room. Everything seemed to be made of stone. Walls, floor, and ceiling were all built of great gray blocks. Even the desk looked as if it had been carved from a boulder.

"Yes, I see you've noticed!" Urrpphh exclaimed with some pride. "I've done the entire place in Modern Rock!"

The demon rested easily on a corner of his great stone desk. "I take great pride in this dungeon. I've built this place up from almost nothing! You saw those words, etched in stone at the entranceway? 'Lose virtually all hope . . .' well, you know the ones. You don't know how much I struggled to get those words. And still they call this dungeon a junior division! I push forward a mile and they give me an inch!"

The demon pointed to one wall of his cavernous office. "Look at the signs I've managed to take down over the years! I keep them all as a measure of my achievement!"

I looked to where he pointed. There were three more of those two-foot-high sentences etched in rock. I quickly scanned the one on top:

LOSE A GREAT DEAL OF YOUR HOPE YE WHO ENTER
HERE

The one immediately below it read:

LOSE SOME OF YOUR HOPE YE WHO ENTER . . .

I didn't even bother to finish the sentence, instead glancing down at the lowest inscription of the three:

YOU MIGHT LOSE A LITTLE BIT OF YOUR HOPE
IF YOU'RE THAT TYPE YE . . .

I looked back up at Urrpphh. I could see his point.

"Yes!" The demon nodded. "And every upgrading was a struggle, let me tell you. You have to keep your thumbscrews perpetually tight, your iron maiden pol-

ished, your oil just about to boil! Real estate! That's all
the Netherhells cares about these days! You have to
fight or they'll take away your pretty jail and put a
Slime-O-Rama in its place. Think about it! Here you
are, a hard-working demon devoting all your life to the
furtherance of pain and suffering. Then one false move
and it's good-bye dungeon, hello Slime Burgers!"

"Indeed," I said when I perceived it was my turn to
speak. "I suppose that's what they call progress?"

"Progress?" Urrpphh grimaced. "Have you ever
tried a Slime Burger? But I forget." He laughed diabol-
ically. "You are a guest here. Soon they will be your
total diet!"

Slime Burgers my total diet? I was beginning to like
this demon's laugh even less. Perhaps he had brought
me here to taunt me, to extend my suffering as long as
possible. Well, I would show him that Wuntvor the apprentice was made of sterner stuff!

"Torture me, then," I cried. "Do your worst! It will
be over soon enough!"

"Oh, no!" The demon's laugh was even more hide-
ous than before. "We don't torture you yet! First it is
time for your agonies!"

Agonies? I didn't like the sound of that at all. Could
there be something worse than torture?

"Come," Urrpphh said solicitously. "We will show
you to your cell."

"Slobber, slobber," the trolls added.

I was once again surrounded by the ill-smelling creatures. There seemed to be no chance of escape. What
had I to look forward to? Torture? Agony? Perhaps, I
wondered, it would be better if I were to provoke one of
these trolls and end it all?

And then I thought of Norei. Where had they taken
her in this vast, strange kingdom? She might even, I
realized, be trapped in this very dungeon. I had come
down into this place where danger lurked at every turn
more to save her than to rescue Vushta. I could admit
that to myself now that I was so close to death. Letting

the trolls eat me was the coward's way out. If there was one chance in a hundred that I might escape, even one chance in a thousand, I owed it to Norei. I was not fighting for only myself now. I was fighting for my beloved!

I gritted my teeth as we entered another low building. "Do your worst," I murmured.

"Oh, don't worry," Urrpphh replied. "We intend to."

The trolls grabbed my arms and dragged me rapidly down a long, circular stone stairway.

"No!" a voice screamed from down below. "Not again! Have you no mercy?"

"Halt, minions!" Urrpphh instructed the bustling trolls. "I want our new guest to see this. It is most instructive as to our methods."

"Slobber!" The trolls pushed me forward so that my face was pressed against the iron bars of a window that looked into a large, well-lit room. The room seemed to be used for purposes of public assembly, for it was filled with rows of benches. At the moment, however, only one man sat in this hall, his form secured to a bench by a dozen thick chains encircling his body. His once fine clothes were torn and caked with blood and his scholarly face was surrounded by a crown of wildly matted hair. He faced a long stage, occupied now by no more than a large yellow sign with ornate, red letters which spelled: "Showtime in two minutes."

"No!" he shrieked. "I can't stand it again!"

"The man you see before you," Urrpphh whispered in my ear, "was once a famed dramatist upon the surface world, producing both wondrous comedy and dire tragedy. Due to a slight error on his part, he signed an agreement with certain demons down below. And we have him now!"

"And you force him to watch plays?" I replied with some relief. "That doesn't sound so bad."

"Bah! There are no plays performed on that stage!"

Urrpphh laughed again. "We force him to watch vaudeville! And it is the worst vaudeville imaginable!"

I blinked. There was a new sign on the stage, larger than the one before, yellow letters on a royal blue background. This one read: "Showtime in one minute!"

"No!" the playwright pleaded. "Please. Please! I cannot take any more!"

"This is a particularly successful agony," Urrpphh said with smug satisfaction. "Few individuals realize the great care we take in producing our agonies, you know. It takes great skill to do it just right. Why, until recently, we not only employed demonic actors and stage technicians, but a full staff of demonic writers to concoct the most horrendous vaudeville routines imaginable!"

"Until recently?" I inquired.

"Yes!" The demon chuckled evilly. "As you may know, we in the Netherhells dungeon business are always on the lookout for efficient cost-cutting measures. Our scouts have located a vaudeville act on the surface world far worse than anything our former writing team could ever come up with! We simply steal this act verbatim, and our guest the dramatist goes through far worse agonies than any he had ever experienced." Urrpphh laughed again even more horribly than before, a sound halfway between that of some large animal retching and water gurgling down a drain.

Perhaps the most bloodcurdling scream I have ever heard issued from the dramatist's throat. He thrashed about wildly in a vain attempt to rearrange his chains so that his bench no longer faced the stage. There was an even larger sign there now, pale green in color with huge, black letters: IT'S SHOWTIME!

"This is *so* bad!" Urrpphh chortled.

A pair of demons trotted out onto the stage. One wore a dress while the other appeared to be garbed in the skin of some large lizard. The two began to sing together:

Wuntvor wasn't much of a wizard,
No ifs, no ands, no buts!
Surely demons drink his blood,
And they've ripped out all his—

"But you have seen enough!" Urrpphh interrupted. "Now it is time for an agony of your very own!"

The dramatist's incoherent screams faded in the distance as the trolls dragged me down the corridor.

"Slobber!" the trolls cried as they opened the cell door at corridor's end.

"Slobber!" they shrieked as they threw me inside.

"Slobber!" they called as they slammed the door behind me and shuffled away.

"Enjoy your suffering!" Urrpphh exclaimed, and then the demon was gone as well.

It was soft where I had landed. I looked up with some trepidation to discern the true nature of my prison. But what was this? It looked as if I were sitting in the midst of a forest glade upon the surface world, the bright midday sun filtered by a roof of green leaves.

I forced my heart to slow, my breathing to become regular. So far this wasn't at all terrible. Perhaps Urrpphh and his minions had made some mistake.

"Wuntvor?" a woman's voice called to me.

My hopes suddenly took wing. Could it be?

A woman appeared between the trees, but it was not Norei. The newcomer was comely enough, with raven tresses and piercing black eyes, but I could not hide my disappointment. Somewhere in the distance I heard faint music play.

"Wuntvor!" the woman pouted. "At last you have come. Why aren't you happy to see me?"

"Excuse me," I replied, still somewhat distracted. "Have we met?"

She laughed, a sound usually reserved for bells of finest silver. "Oh, that is it! You toy with your beloved!" She walked toward me over the soft earth that was strewn with pine needles. "Still, you have met me at our favorite spot, here by our forest bed."

Forest bed? What was she talking about? Had this woman been sent here to entice me? Well, she was certainly beautiful. But no! I was true to Norei. I would not fall victim to some Netherhells trick! I noticed that strange music again. It seemed to have grown louder.

"Oh, Wuntvor!" the woman cooed as she reached my side. "You are so tense. Here. Allow me to relax you." She stood before me and placed one long-fingered hand on each of my shoulders, then gazed deep into my eyes. I did not find it relaxing. Why was my mouth so dry? Wasn't that music getting louder?

"Wuntvor," the raven-haired woman whispered. "You don't know how long I've waited, nay, how long I've dreamed about this moment. Oh, how I burn for your kiss!"

Yes, I was sure the music was louder now. It surrounded us both and made it difficult to think. What was happening? Was it the Netherhells Buying Fever again? But there was nothing here to buy. My, but this woman's eyes were awfully large. I hadn't really noticed how attractive her lips were, either. I was finding it difficult to breathe, also.

"Oh, Wuntvor," the woman sighed, and my name on her lips was the most wonderful sound in the world. "Oh," she moaned, "Wuntvor! Take me!"

Yes, I would! Yes! Anything she wanted! Yes! Her hands moved across my shoulder blades to draw me near to her. Yes! Our faces grew close, our lips closer still. Yes! Yes! Yes!

"Daughter?" cried a voice gruffer than that of the trolls.

I kissed empty air. My raven-haired beauty had pulled away.

"Oh, woe!" she moaned. "It is my father, who is sworn to kill any man who might love me. You are so brave, Wuntvor, to love me as you do, knowing that my father is the greatest swordsman in all of the kingdom. But hark! He comes through the trees!''

There was a great rustling just out of sight, as if not one swordsman, but an entire army, approached.

''Run, my beloved, run, or he shall skewer your liver!'' My raven-haired beauty leaned over to kiss me, but then thought better of it. She pushed me into the trees opposite the approaching sounds of her father.

I ran until I reached another clearing. I paused to gain my breath as best I could, to run farther if need be, but I heard no sounds of pursuit.

It was only then that I had time to think about what had happened to me.

Who was that raven-haired beauty? What had she wanted from me? Even though we had only just met, my lips still ached for her kiss and my arms still yearned for her embrace.

I shook myself. Why wasn't I thinking of Norei? I remembered the music then, swelling all about me, carrying both me and my new lover to heights of anticipation. It had to be another Netherhells trick! Well, whatever they were doing to me, I knew of their foul plans now. I would not let it happen again!

Something warm covered my eyes.

''Guess who, Wuntvor?'' a woman's voice said. She removed her hands from my face and I turned to see a woman with hair blonder than Alea's.

''Do I know you?'' I asked. Did I hear that music again in the distance?

''Oh, so you are playing games with me as well!'' The woman laughed. ''I know a game we can play!''

So the Netherhells would try the same trick! No, this time I knew! Somehow I had to get out of this trap and find Norei, my true beloved! I began to turn away.

''Why do you not answer me, sweet one?'' the blond woman pouted. She grabbed hold of my arm with surprising strength. I looked back into the deepest blue eyes I had ever seen.

No! I would remember Norei! The blond woman

took my chin between her thumb and forefinger. Yes, the music was definitely there! I could almost make out the melody!

"Ah, that is more like it," the beautiful woman said. She was using her other hand to stroke the back of my neck at the bottom of my hair line. It made chills pass through my whole being. I was supposed to remember somebody, wasn't I? Or something? Oh, who cared! All I needed to remember were my beloved's eyes, my beloved's lips, and my beloved's hair.

I leaned forward to kiss her.

"Where are you, wife?"

"Oh, no!" the blond cried, leaping away from me. "We are discovered! I knew we should stop meeting like this! But you were so insistent, even though my husband is the greatest archer in the kingdom! Oh, how could I resist!"

An arrow embedded itself in a tree by my left ear.

"He has seen us!" The blond shuddered. "Oh, Wuntvor, my husband is such a vengeful man! After he shoots you, he will have you drawn and quartered! Oh, run, Wuntvor! Run for your life!"

Another arrow whizzed close by my right ear. I turned and took my beloved's advice, although it meant we could never fulfill our love.

I stopped running after a moment. What was I thinking of? What love? Norei! That was who I was supposed to remember. It was so hard to think with that music playing!

"Wuntvor!" a woman's voice called from the woods before me. "What a surprise!"

Oh, no. I wouldn't let this happen to me again! I would turn and run, somewhere where there were not all these women constantly hounding me.

And then the third woman stepped out from between the trees. She had red hair, just as Norei had red hair. But Norei's hair was dull by comparison. This woman's hair was the color of flame!

"Wuntvor!" she cried. "Do not reject me!"

I could hear the music building behind me. If I did not escape now, I knew it would be too late! "Excuse me," I said without conviction. "I have something I have to do—er—in another part of the forest."

The beautiful red-headed woman walked quickly up to me and threw me to the ground. "Wuntvor!" she repeated. "Do not reject me!"

And seeing her this close, how could I? Those perfect lips, those eyes the color of the sea. Why had I wanted to run away from her? I let her pull me up to her by my shirt front, let the music swell around us, binding us together. We would be as one forever! I needed to take her to my den!

"Lunch time!" came a voice from behind me.

I heard a door slam against a wall. They had opened my cell! I had quite forgotten I was in a cell.

"Beloved!" I murmured to the beautiful red-headed woman. Her lips were so close to mine!

There was a roar in the distance.

"Oh, no!" she said. "It is my intended, who through enchantment has been turned into the most fearsome fire-breathing dragon in all the kingdom! He swore, if ever I was to even kiss a man before—"

"Slobber!" A troll grabbed my arm and pulled me away from my rapidly-speaking love.

"W-what?" I stammered as Urrpphh's face suddenly loomed before me. "Who?" I shook my head, but it was as if I could not awaken. Why didn't they stop that too-loud music? "Where?"

"Sorry you got pulled away midembrace, huh?" the demon smirked. "Pardon me. It was really *almost* midembrace, wasn't it? Well, you'll have plenty more of the same opportunities, believe me. But for now, you have to eat. You need to keep up your strength, you know!"

The troll dragged me toward a table set for one. On the place before me was a sea of gray muck surrounding two slices of soggy bread.

"This is a real occasion," Urrpphh chortled. "You're about to eat your very first Slime Burger!"

Slime Burger? They expected me to eat Slime Burgers? This, at last, was too much. Even the Netherhells could only push Wuntvor the apprentice so far. I struggled mightly in the troll's grasp.

The troll calmly flipped me over its shoulder and began to carry me toward the offending meal. Two things fell from my pocket: a piece of parchment and a small, red card.

The troll picked up the card.

"No slobber!" it squealed in terror.

"Let me see that!" Urrpphh demanded. The troll got rid of the card as if it burned its fingers.

"Why, you . . ." Urrpphh began, almost beside himself with rage. "How did you get—" He stopped with visible effort, staring at the card, and then turned his hate-filled gaze straight at me.

"Get out of here!"

Yes! It was so obvious! Why hadn't I thought of it! There were the words of the card, in bold, block letters: GET OUT OF JAIL FREE!

The door to my cell opened of its own accord. They were letting me go! I would not question my good fortune. I moved rapidly out the door and down the corridor.

"No!" the dramatist screamed as I passed. "Not an encore! Anything but an encore!"

But I could spare nothing but a moment's pity for the poor, doomed soul. Through a stroke of either luck or my master's foresight I had been spared from almost certain madness. And I had been given another chance to find my beloved Norei and save Vushta in the bargain!

"Slobber!" the trolls yelled behind me. "Slobber!"

They sounded close behind me. Too close. Were they following me?

"Of course, once you are beyond the dungeon

walls," Urrpphh called after me, "there is nothing to keep us from taking you prisoner again." He laughed demonically. "But this time you will no longer have the card!"

I distinctly heard a rip. The rip of a small, red card, without doubt.

Huge hounds barked down at me from the parapets. The main gate opened before me barely wide enough to let me pass between its crimson spikes.

"Slobber!" the trolls chorused, even closer now than before. "Slobber!"

I stepped beyond the spiked gate to freedom. I thought I felt hot troll breath upon my neck. I began to run through the spongy glowing moss with every ounce of strength I had remaining.

"Slobber!" a troll sounded in my ear.

How long could I stay free? I had to escape, for my master, for Vushta, and my beloved.

"Norei!" I cried as I ran.

And someone answered me.

# TWELVE

*Reunions can be a wonderful thing, especially when neither of the reunited parties manage to recall what separated them in the first place.*

—*from* The Teachings of Ebenezum,
Wizard's Digest Condensed edition

"Slobber!"

"Slobber! Slobber!"

There were trolls on either side of me!

"Wuntvor!" the voice called to me again from up ahead. It couldn't be! And yet it was!

"Norei!" I shouted with every bit of breath left in my lungs.

And then the trolls grabbed me.

"Slobber! Slobber! Slobber!"

They surrounded me. There must have been a dozen or more of them! Large, hairy hands grabbed my arms and legs and hair. The trolls began to drag me back toward the dungeon.

I felt a cold wind blow all about me. The trolls stopped in their tracks.

"Slobber!" the trolls cried in confusion. "No slobber!"

I looked up as the trolls loosened their grip upon my body. Where were we? I couldn't tell in what direction the trolls had been dragging me, nor could I tell quite where I had been.

Then it occurred to me. Norei must be using a misdirection spell! Maybe this would give me a chance to escape. Summoning my remaining strength, I jerked free of the last troll's grasp. I would run to my beloved witch! Together we would turn back the trolls and rescue Vushta in the bargain.

But which way was Norei? I could barely distinguish between up and down, let alone right, left, forward, and back!

"Norei!" I cried out to the chaos.

"Wuntvor!" she called back and the spell was broken for me. My beloved stood a mere fifty paces farther down the corridor! I ran, calling her name again.

"Slobber!"

I was seized again by hairy hands. Unfortunately, when the spell broke for me, it also broke for the trolls as well. I felt myself being pulled back toward the dungeon.

"Norei!" I shouted, more than a tinge of panic in my voice.

A warm wind blew by us all.

"Slobber!" the confused trolls cried again. "No slobber!" The ground seemed to have turned to mud, sucking their feet within so they could not move. But how could I escape? My feet were disappearing into the mud as well!

"Wuntvor!" Norei called as she ran up to the edge of the muddy morass. " 'Tis but a temporary hindrance spell. There are too many trolls here. I will need to think of something really powerful to set you free!"

"Norei!" I responded. "I have faith in you!"

"Good. I believe we can use all the faith we have." My beloved frowned, as if concentrating on the next spell she would use. She flung out her hands and shouted a dozen words.

A wind of near-searing heat blew past me and the trolls.

"No slobber!" the trolls began to cry in panic. The powerful spell spun them about and pressed them to the mud.

But my beloved had miscalculated. The heat from this new spell was so great that it began to dry the morass entrapping my captors' feet. One by one, they began to pull themselves free of the imprisoning muck.

"Slobber!" one said tentatively.

"Slobber! Slobber!" another added with much greater authority.

I once again found myself grasped by a myriad of troll hands.

"No!" I protested.

A bunch of flowers fell out of my shirt.

What? For an instant, my confused mind searched for meaning in the daisies about my feet. Then I remembered the hat. Norei had told me it might be reactivated during periods of extreme magic! And there was extreme magic all about me now!

"Yes!" I cried.

A bunch of scarves fell into the mud.

The wind buffeted the trolls back again. Some of them even lost their hold upon my person. Oddly enough, I did not feel the wind as strongly as I had before. Somehow, Norei was modulating her spell so that it affected the trolls much more than it affected me!

Still, though, it was not enough for the trolls to release me completely from their collective death grip. However, what would happen if there were some further distraction? It was certainly worth the attempt. Perhaps it just might work!

"Perhaps!" I shouted. "Perhaps! Perhaps! Perhaps! Perhaps and perhaps!"

"Eep!

"Eep eep eep!"

"Eep eep eep eep eep!"

An army of ferrets leaped from my shirt front.

The trolls were overwhelmed. The wind spell alone they might have weathered. The ferrets by themselves they would probably have laughed at. But the two together were far too much for the trolls' small brains to deal with.

"No slobber!" the trolls shrieked. "No slobber!" Covered with ferrets, they beat a hasty retreat to the dungeon gate.

I found myself suddenly troll-free.

"Norei!" I called. I ran, as best as I could, into the arms of my beloved.

"Oh, Wuntvor," Norei chided as she pushed away from me. "I know you are glad to see me, but we are still in dire peril!"

I regarded my beloved with some concern. She looked much more worn than I had ever seen her before.

"Oh, I am quite all right!" She smiled weakly as she saw the concern on my face. "I'm just a little tired. It took all of my magical skills to help free you from the trolls. Now I need to recover. Our current position is too well known by the forces of the Netherhells! We must leave this place as quickly and quietly as possible."

I had Norei lean against me as we turned to walk up the corridor that would lead us back to the Netherhells mall. With my beloved by my side, I felt my own strength return every time I took a step. Together we would persevere!

"Wuntvor!" Norei cried with alarm. "There's something coming!"

She was right! There was a sound like two hundred small feet pounding against the phosphorescent moss.

"Eep!"

"Eep eep!"

Dozens of small, furry things rushed to follow us. With the trolls gone, the ferrets had begun to gather around me again.

"Eep eep! Eep eep!"

"Well," Norei amended as we picked our way through the gladly crying, nuzzling horde. "At least we can go quickly."

There seemed to be no signs of pursuit as we moved rapidly along the glowing green corridor. I asked Norei how she had managed to get away.

"Easy enough," she answered. "Once that short, loud demon left the Collectors, it was simplicity itself to hit them with a confusion spell and simply walk out of their claws. The Collectors are vicious, but they are not very bright.''

That was my Norei, ready for any challenge! I kissed her chastely upon the cheek.

"Oh, Wuntvor!" Norei frowned again. "Is that all you can think of at a time like this? Here we are, still in dire peril, waiting for perhaps the entire might of the Netherhells to descend upon us, and I am stuck walking down a corridor with an amorous apprentice and his three-score trained ferrets!''

"Norei?" I whispered, quite taken aback. "If you feel that way, why did you rescue me?''

My beloved glanced at me and her exhausted countenance broke into a genuine smile. "Oh, you know how I feel about you, you big oaf. It's only that your behavior isn't always as appropriate to the situation as it might be!" She glanced at her feet. "Besides, it's annoying having to look down constantly so you won't trip over a ferret!''

I smiled, filled with an inner peace. What did it matter what befell us now, so long as we were together? My beloved loved me still!

"Wait!" Norei placed a cautionary hand upon my shoulder. "I sense someone ahead."

I looked beyond the sea of ferrets that surrounded us. We had come almost to the end of the corridor. I could see the window displays of the stores mere paces before me. But something was wrong. There were no beckoning torches lit to lure unwary customers, and those stores I could see clearly were dark inside. It looked like a Netherhells trap. Oh, what I would do for a weapon now, even Cuthbert, my cowardly sword!

"There they are!" a voice cried from the gloom ahead. "Doom!"

Five figures stepped into the space where the corridor met the mall.

"Who?" Norei fell back automatically into a basic conjuring position.

"Hold!" I cautioned her. "I believe these are our compatriots."

"Wuntvor?" a timorous voice inquired. "Could it be you?"

I noticed then that the tallest of those before us held aloft a gently glowing sword.

"Yes, it is I!" I called in return. "And I have brought Norei with me!"

"Oh, Wuntvor! Wuntvor!" Cuthbert yelped with glee. "I'm so glad to see you! Now I can be returned to my rightful master! You don't know what a trial it's been to be possessed by this big fellow in black!" Cuthbert shivered in the Dealer's hands. "Why, he wants to fight all the time!"

The Dealer smiled at that. "We've been hewing demons of late."

"Oh, hew, hew, hew!" Cuthbert wailed. "He had me cutting anything and everything! There was ichor flying everywhere!"

"Yes," the Dealer agreed. "It was quite lovely, wasn't it?"

Zzzzz the demon stepped forward, a large grin upon his wizened face. "We've been revitalizing!"

"Doom!" Hendrek added.

"Oh, give me back to Wuntvor!" Cuthbert pleaded. "I showed you where to find him. What else could you ask a magic sword to do?"

"Well . . ." the Dealer began.

"I know! I know!" the sword wailed. "But it is Wuntvor who should decide! After all, I was given to him by the wizards!"

"Oh, all right,'" the Dealer said with some reluctance. He handed Cuthbert and the scabbard to me. "It's back to strangling, then. But it's become so boring. I mean, where's the sport?"

"You were whistling a different tune when you met the Collectors!" Snarks remarked. "It isn't such a piece of cake when your victims have no necks!"

"Snarks?" I questioned. "You're still here?"

"You mean, after betraying you?" The demon waved his hands about in a helpless gesture. "You know I couldn't help myself. I have to tell the truth, no matter what the cost!"

"Doom!" Hendrek remarked. "Then he and Brax went off and joined the forces of the Netherhells!"

Snarks took a step backwards. "Well, it was sort of expected of us. Here we were, with the Collectors staring us in the face, and if we weren't against them, we had to be with them!"

"Yeah!" Brax stepped forward, waving his cigar. "But wait 'til you hear what we found out! Have we got a deal for you!"

"You!" Norei said in a voice filled with ice.

"Beg pardon?" Brax turned to the young witch. "Oh, the woman we absconded with. I didn't recognize you. You should hit me on the head once or twice. Then I'd know you right away!"

"What is this fiend doing in our midst?" Norei demanded.

"Now hold onto your spells there for a moment!" Brax chided. "Who do you think made it possible for you to escape? Rule number one of the successful sales supervisor: Never leave Collectors out on their own! Without proper supervision, those fellows can't collect their way out of a paper bag!"

"So you allowed me to escape?" Norei's voice was heavy with sarcasm. "I have you to thank for everything?"

"No question about it," Brax replied. "I couldn't be too obvious, you know. If I just said, 'Okay, lady, time to escape!' it would have blown my cover sky high!"

"Don't be too harsh on him," Snarks added. "I know he's a worthless salesdemon, and I have yet to discover any of his good points, but he did have his uses. Between the two of us, we discovered the whereabouts of Vushta!"

I looked back and forth between Brax and Snarks. Could we truly trust these demons?

"Listen," Snarks said when he saw my skepticism. "Let me tell you everything that happened, so you can see I haven't really changed and I'm still the sincere, truthful demon that I always was!"

I looked to the others in our party.

"You are wondering, perhaps, why these demons are still alive?" the Dealer asked. "I had decided to wait a bit before I kill them. We are in a strange place among strange creatures. I thought it best not to strangle them until we had time for some discussion." The large man flexed his hands absently. "In addition, you know the way I feel about demons." The Dealer made a muscular face. "They squish."

"Doom," added Hendrek.

"Revitalize them all!" Zzzzz cried. "Oh, when they tore down my home to build a Slime-O-Rama, I never realized it would be so much fun!"

"Hold it right there!" Snarks protested. "I never wanted to be involved in this in the first place. I could have spent the rest of my life in relative happiness, worshiping an extremely minor deity at Heemat's retreat. But no, I get dragged along with you folks to save the world!"

"Doom," Hendrek remarked again. "The demon is right. Let him speak his piece."

"Good," Snarks replied, his voice a good deal calmer than before. "I'm glad to see at least one human shows a little common sense. So here we are, confronted by Collectors, demanding to know if we are for or against the Netherhells! Well, what could we say?"

"I told them about the Netherhells that used to be!" Brax said, patriotic fervor once again rising in his voice. "The quiet beauty of a lava flow at night, the pristine cries of the perpetually tormented, the glorious feeling when you get up in the morning and fill your lungs with that first breath of fetid waste! That's what the Netherhells is all about!"

"And I kept my mouth shut," Snarks added. "Brax was doing enough talking for the both of us!"

"But wait!" I interjected. "There were three demons here. What happened to Zzzzz?"

"They ignored me," the elder demon answered. "They always ignore me. Everybody always ignores me. Revitalize them all!"

"To continue with my story," Snarks said quickly, "the Collectors told us to go to this demonic aid station just up the road—"

"And may I add," Brax put in, "when the Collectors tell you to do something, you do it!"

"If I might?" Snarks remarked peremptorily. "Thank you. Anyway, we thought it best to comply with the Collectors' request. And I must admit that I had a further motive. The Netherhells, after all, was where I was born and raised, and I harbored some lingering homesickness for what I used to know!"

"The feel of burning sulfur beneath your feet!" Brax rhapsodized. "The joyous agony of being bathed, head to foot, in slime!"

"If you don't mind!" Snarks spoke haughtily to his fellow demon. "Thank you. Is there anyone here who wishes to add anything further? No? Very good. I shall proceed."

The demon cleared his throat. "As I was saying, I felt some nostalgia for the Netherhells that was. We were going to a place where demons rested and recovered from their ills. Perhaps, I thought, there would be a park where the old ways were still preserved. I could see a sulfur pool or two, maybe a bit of flowing magma. But no!"

Brax seemed about to speak. Snarks glared at him for an instant before he continued.

"I think I realized from the first that I would never find an answer to my longing. But this!" The demon shuddered. "The aid station was indistinguishable from the rest of the mall, full of multicolored torches, and that faint, insidious music urging us on. I found myself wanting to wrap myself in bandages, or use half a dozen crutches simultaneously! And then the worst hap-

pened . . ." Snarks paused, as if what occurred next was
almost too horrible to remember.

The demon took a deep breath. "They fed us Slime
Burgers!" he managed at last.

"Ah, yes!" Brax intoned, the patriotic fervor still in
his voice. "It's not like the Netherhells cuisine of yes-
teryear. Remember how good a real Sweet Demon Pie
tastes? Ah, the way those brambles stick to your gums!"

Indeed," I remarked. "But you mentioned that you
had found a way to Vushta?"

Snarks nodded. "Vushta, it appears, is all the talk
among demonkind. What they see in a dull city full of
human beings is beyond me! Then again, anything must
be better than life in an intercity mall!"

Now that Snarks had confessed his transgression, the
acid tone was once again flowing back into his voice. He
sounded just like the demon that we knew and . . . Well,
he sounded just like the demon that we knew. Perhaps
Snarks had been telling the truth all along.

"Anyway," the demon continued, "they've trans-
ported Vushta to the city of Upper Retch, Netherhells
knows why. And, according to a chart on the station
wall, there is a passageway that will lead us directly to
that city a mere few minutes' walk from here!"

So we were closer to Vushta than I had thought. We
might triumph yet!

"Indeed," I said. "Then we are nearing our destination. What say we get on with it?"

The others in our party agreed that it was time to go.

"Doom," Hendrek added as we began to march. "I
still carry your horn." He handed me the sack that contained Wonk, the horn of persuasion. I tied it to my belt
opposite Cuthbert's scabbard.

"What are these?" The Dealer of Death looked at my
army of ferrets. There seemed to be a strange longing in
his eyes.

"So soft," he whispered, "so warm. They're not
much like a wild pig, but they're more like a wild pig
than a demon is!" The Dealer looked at me hopefully.

"You wouldn't mind if I strangled just one?"

I looked over the sea of brown that followed our procession. "I would very much! These are my ferrets!"

"Yes, I suppose you are right." The Dealer sighed. "I know I should only strangle for a cause. But I can't help myself! How was I to know wild pigs would become addictive?"

I was troubled as well. Only with the Dealer's question had I come to realize how much my ferrets meant to me.

"Here we are!" Snarks shouted.

"Doom!" Hendrek cried, warclub at the ready. "Where?"

Brax and Snarks struggled together to lift a large plate from the ground.

"On the road to Vushta!" Snarks explained.

I walked to the edge of the hole they had uncovered. It appeared to be some sort of chute, going straight down.

"Here?" I asked, a bit of doubt in my voice.

Snarks nodded. "Upper Retch is directly below our current location."

"Upper Retch is below us?" I asked. Had I accepted the demons back among us too soon!? Was this some sort of Netherhells trick?

"I'm afraid so." Snarks smiled happily.

"Then why do they call it Upper—"

"It's the way demons think," Snarks replied. "Down you go!"

With that, the demon gave me a hearty push.

I yelped as I fell in the hole, sliding down the chute into darkness.

# THIRTEEN

*When there appears to be no hope; when all around you are screaming like lost souls and every spell you try fails to work; when it appears that chaos and evil will at last triumph over good—then it is truly time for a vacation.*

—*from* The Teachings of Ebenezum,
*Volume XXXV*

I dropped at what seemed to be tremendous speed through total blackness. I heard other noises above me. One sounded like a woman's yell, another a deep-throated "Doom" that reverberated down the shaft. Could the demons have thrown my compatriots down the chute as well?

The sides of the passageway through which I slid were utterly sleek. There seemed no chance of me finding a handhold to stop or even slow my progress. I heard a cry of terror. I thought for a moment that it came from my own throat, until I realized it really came from the scabbard at my belt. For the briefest instant I considered drawing Cuthbert to throw some light on this total gloom, but I was traveling so fast that I feared the sword would be torn from my grasp. I was falling so rapidly now that I would surely be crushed the next time I hit something solid. I silently apologized to my master for dying in such a stupid way and consequently being unable to rescue Vushta.

Then, as suddenly as I had dropped into darkness, I found myself flying through the strange greenish glow of the Netherhells. I landed in a huge pile of phosphorescent moss, then tumbled down to rest where the moss met the floor of the cave.

"Doo—oof!" came the cry above me. I quickly

scrambled out of the way to avoid the great bulk now rolling down the mossy slope. I heard Norei's cheerful yell as I stood up and brushed myself off, then looked up to see the Dealer's large form sail silently through the air. Three small figures followed in rapid succession, the demons Zzzzz, Brax, and Snarks.

Then perhaps this wasn't a Netherhells plot! But then exactly what was going on?

"Gangway!" Snarks said, leaping from the top of the mossy pile. "Ferrets coming through!"

The sky rained small, brown furry things.

"Good!" Snarks exclaimed as he looked about. "Looks like everyone's accounted for."

"Ah," Brax said with a grin. "The Netherhells express. I ask you—is there any other way to travel?"

I approached the cigar-smoking demon. "Is that what it's called? The Netherhells express?"

"What else would you call it?" Brax said with some surprise.

"I could think of a couple things," I replied. "But that's beside the point. Why didn't you warn us what was going to happen?"

"Would you have jumped as readily into that hole if we did?" Snarks reasoned.

"Besides," Brax confided, "we heard voices from farther down the corridor. Three voices talking in unison."

"The Dread Collectors!" the Dealer of Death rumbled.

"Yeah!" Zzzzz broke in. "I wanted to stay there and revitalize them!"

"But you know what happened the last time we attempted to fight the Collectors," Snarks reminded us. "So we decided that rescuing Vushta was more important."

"Vushta!" I repeated the name of that fabled city and the old wonder crept back into my voice. "Are we near?"

"If my calculations are correct," Snarks said, "and

they always are, we should be able to see Vushta as soon as we climb the next rise!"

So I would see Vushta at last!

"Maybe it is time to contact Ebenezum," Norei suggested.

She was right. We were about to enter Vushta and confront the dread Guxx Unfufadoo. Now was the moment we really needed the wizard's expertise.

I drew Cuthbert from its scabbard.

"What!" the sword screamed. "You don't need me already, do you? I still haven't recovered from all the hewing that big fellow did!"

I explained to the sword in my calmest tone that we needed to contact the wizard Ebenezum.

"Oh. Why didn't you say so? I can be quite reasonable, if properly informed. But no, you let me go on and on . . ."

"You know," I mentioned to Norei, "I could give this sword back to the Dealer."

"Magical communication!" the sword cried. "Magic you want, magic you get! Coming right up! We aim to please, yes, sir!"

"Indeed," I replied. "We need to talk with Ebenezum again, in East Vushta."

"My extreme pleasure!" Cuthbert answered. "You know the routine. Swing away!"

I swung the sword three times, until the point of light had again become a window to the surface world.

This time, the window opened on the interior of the extension school, perhaps the front hallway. The image blurred and shifted and we were in the Great Hall.

"In theory," Snorphosio shouted, "there is no reason why our plan to save Vushta won't—"

"Theory, hah!" Zimplitz retorted. "Magic is only proved through practice! Before a spell can truly work, it has to be baptized in a magician's blood!

"If what you are saying was true, Vushta would be littered with dead magicians. Only through theory can—"

I cleared my throat. "Excuse me."

Both magicians' heads snapped around to the window.

"What!" Snorphosio cried.

"Why, 'tis the apprentice!" Zimplitz waved in my direction.

"I see it's the apprentice," Snorphosio rejoined peevishly. "I was just wondering what he wanted!"

Zimplitz smiled cruelly. "You were wondering what he wanted in theory, eh?"

"I will not have you make fun of my craft!" Snorphosio screamed. "I am more than capable of talking with the apprentice! Why don't you go outside and play some of your dirty little magic tricks!"

"Dirty!" Zimplitz fumed. "Little! Why, you . . ."

The magicians grappled with each other and fell upon the floor.

"Excuse me," I tried again.

"Yes, yes, be with you in a second!" one of them hollered.

"If this fool would just listen to reason!" the other retorted. With them rolling about the floor like that, it was difficult to tell them apart.

"Please!" I called. "Just answer one question. Where is my master, Ebenezum?"

One of the mages pulled free of the other's grasp. As he dusted himself off, I saw he was Snorphosio.

"Ebenezum sits on the dais behind—ulp!" Snorphosio fell as Zimplitz grabbed him around the knees. I looked above the two struggling sorcerers to the dais. Yes, there was my master, still wearing his worn and tattered robes. He lay full out upon the marble. He appeared to be sound asleep.

"Master!" I called.

Ebenezum snored peacefully.

"Let me try," Cuthbert suggested cheerfully. He emitted a loud whistle. "Oh, magician!"

There was no response from the sleeping mage.

"No," the Dealer of Death said from behind me.

"You need something really loud to wake a mage from so profound a sleep." He made a sound like a dozen bull elephants engaged in a screaming contest.

My master rolled on his side and snored even louder.

"There is only one way to wake the mage!" Norei informed us. "We must all shout as one!"

All of us screamed together, our noise echoed by the squeals of sixty exuberant ferrets.

My master scratched absently at one eyebrow. His snoring continued unabated.

It was a dire problem; so close to Vushta and unable to confer with the greatest magician in all the Western Kingdoms. What could I do to wake my master? Even our combined shouting was not enough. What could possibly be loud enough to break through my master's slumbers?

Then the answer came to me.

"Cover your ears," I told the others. "I fear I will have to use Wonk."

The magicians stopped wrestling.

"Wonk?" they both cried.

"Oh, you need to wake your master!" Zimplitz exclaimed, as if it were the most novel idea in the world.

"Let us do it for you!" Snorphosio was all smiles as well.

"Yes, we'll be more than happy to!" Zimplitz climbed the steps to the left of the dais.

"All you have to do is ask. After all, you're the hero around here." Snorphosio climbed the steps to the right.

Snorphosio and Zimplitz each shook one of Ebenezum's shoulders.

"No, no," the magician mumbled. "I know they look like rats but—What? What is the matter?" The mage sat up as both Zimplitz and Snorphosio pointed toward the magic window.

"Wuntvor!" My master smiled as he rubbed the sleep from his eyes. "You've contacted us again!"

Ebenezum yawned. "Excuse me. I had the strangest dream. The world had become overrun with ferrets. But we don't have time to discuss that now. You must have called for a reason."

I told my master that indeed I had. We had reached the outskirts of Vushta and wanted to tell those above about our current position.

"Also," I added, "we would not frown on any last-minute advice you might have to offer."

"Indeed," Ebenezum said. "I am glad that you have been able to keep in touch. Knowing you are so close to your goal will help facilitate the final plan. So far, you seem to have done well enough. Is that the Dealer of Death I see behind you? No, don't explain. There will be time enough for explanations when Vushta is back where it belongs. Be sure to follow the original instructions and I'm sure everything will go splendidly."

I quickly went over the plan in my head. I was to locate Guxx and, through the use of the special spell Ebenezum had given me, along with my magic weapons, I was to remove a single nose hair from the demon's proboscis. It seemed simple enough in theory. To maximize our chances, I should take time beforehand to memorize the spell.

"Oh, tell him about Klothus!" Snorphosio giggled.

"Indeed," Ebenezum frowned. "I do not think this is the time to go into—"

"Your master may be a qualified wizard," Zimplitz called to me, "but sometimes he can be a little reserved. Let me tell the story. It seems that Klothus, miffed at his lack of success in clothing your master, insisted that he could make ducks and bunnies look somewhat like moons and stars!"

"It was not a pretty sight!" Snorphosio added.

"What!" I asked. "The ducks and bunnies?"

"No, no," Snorphosio chortled. "Klothus, when your master was done!"

"I wanted to tell him about that!" Zimplitz yelled.

Snorphosio laughed. "Well, for once you weren't quite fast enough, were you? And you call yourself the Action Wizard!"

"I've had enough of you!" Zimplitz shrieked. "I'm going to cram all your theories down your throat!" Once again he leaped for the skinny wizard.

Alea walked into the room, stepping around the two mages rolling on the floor. She spoke to Ebenezum:

"Hubert seeks an audience. He has a few new verses for the song. Oh, hello, Wuntie—"

The picture blinked out.

"I told you about vaudeville," Cuthbert said curtly.

I had had enough of this sword. I twirled Cuthbert back toward where the Dealer stood.

"Then again," the sword said, "perhaps I've never given vaudeville the chance it truly deserves."

"So she still calls you Wuntie." Norei gazed at me icily.

Perhaps, I thought, I should curb my anger. Cuthbert may have eliminated the window at the best possible moment.

"On to Vushta!" I cried. "We cannot falter now!"

We began the march up the hill where we would first see the city of a thousand forbidden delights.

There was a loud noise behind us. I turned. It was coming from the chute Brax had termed the Netherhells express. It took me a moment to realize it was voices echoing down the shaft. They seemed to be saying one thing over and over again.

I paused, attempting to make it out.

"We we we come come come to to to col col col lect lect lect."

"Doom!" Hendrek shouted.

I waved at the others to follow me. It appeared that we would enter Vushta at something more than a stately walk.

# FOURTEEN

*When one first arrives in Vushta, one should beware of street sellers offering forbidden delights near the outskirts of town. These first delights are far more shoddy in nature than those to be had in the inner City, and can be actively unpleasant if you do not have an affinity for goats.*

—*from* Vushta on Twenty-five Pieces of Gold a Day *by Ebenezum, Greatest Wizard in the Western Kingdoms, revised, updated fourth edition*

We were too close to our goal to be stopped by the Dread Collectors! I reached the top of the hill, the rest of the party on my heels.

And I saw Vushta.

I wish that I had had time to stand there and savor it. I saw glimpses of multicolored pastel towers as I ran, structures that appeared to be three times taller than anything I had seen, even in East Vushta! A dozen banners rose above the city walls, as bright in color as the towers were subtle. And there seemed to be people everywhere on the city's winding streets!

I learned a valuable lesson bounding down that hill: It is very difficult to gape and escape at the same time. Could I help it if Vushta's magnificence filled my eyes so that I could not watch my feet? Somewhere about halfway down the hill I found something they could not bound across. I tripped and swiftly rolled to the city gate.

"Hey, watch it there, fella!" a tall, rather unkempt man shouted as he scurried out of my way.

I apologized as I rose to my feet. A quick check

showed that I still carried both my weapons.

"Doo—oof!" Hendrek cried as he, too, rolled to a spot not far from where I had landed.

"Are there more where you come from?" The unkempt man squinted up the hill.

"There's a few," I replied, "but I think they'll all be on foot."

The Dealer of Death reached us next, his great legs leaping more than running down the hillside. He pulled up next to us, breathing as if he had merely had a summer stroll.

"Sorry I am late," he apologized, "but I do not like to roll."

Norei arrived next, followed by the three demons.

"Good heavens!" the unkempt man exclaimed. "Are you a tour group?"

"Indeed," I said. If we could put this Vushta native at ease, perhaps we could get some information from him. "After a fashion."

"Say." The man smiled. Half his teeth seemed to be gone. "Have you ever seen a forbidden delight?"

"Indeed," I said. "I understand there are a thousand of them within these city walls."

"More or less," the man agreed. "But most of them aren't as interesting as one I know. Would you like to come and see?"

I frowned. "Well, perhaps later, if we have the time. I have to wait for the rest of our group to arrive."

"The rest of your group?" The unkempt man rubbed his hands together in anticipation.

"Indeed," I answered. "Here they come now. You can hear their cries as they top the hill."

"Eep!"

"Eep eep!"

"Eep eep eep!"

Our little companions swept down the hill like some great, brown wave.

"Ferrets?" The unkempt man looked at the hill in horror. "You travel with ferrets?"

"Indeed," I replied. "In fact, in a way we are personally related. Now, about this forbidden delight—"

"Forget it!" the man stated as he walked away. "I can see I misjudged you. You're way out of my league. Ferrets? Personally related? Maybe you'll find something to your taste inside those walls. But I think you're going to have to go all the way to the Inner City!"

"Indeed?" I said to the man's rapidly retreating back. I turned to the others. "I had heard that Vushta was different. Apparently the natives here have strange customs. We shall have to do better with the next person we meet."

The ferrets at our heels, we walked through the great gates that led into Vushta.

A short, fat man walked our way. "Ah hah, I perceive you are strangers!" he called. "Have you ever seen a forbidden delight?"

I explained to this man that we were new to town.

"I thought so!" the man chortled. "And I imagine you'd like somebody who can show you around? Well, fortune has smiled upon you today. Honest Emir is at your service!"

"Honest Emir?" Brax muttered darkly. I realized that our demonic companion, in his guise as used weapons seller, had often attached the word "honest" to his name as well. Perhaps Brax was aware of the word's true and inner meaning, at least in a business context.

"Eep!"

"Eep eep!"

"Eep eep eep!"

Three-score ferrets ran rapidly through the gate, all crying with joy that they had found me again.

"What is this?" Honest Emir's belly shook as he laughed. "So you are new to town and you just happen to be traveling with an army of ferrets! Now who is fooling who?"

I opened my mouth to speak, but I was not quite sure what to say. Once again we seemed to be having problems communicating. It must have something to do with living in a large city. Perhaps words common in the countryside took on an entirely different meaning among the urban throngs.

I decided the best thing to do was to be as truthful as possible.

"Indeed," I began in a low voice. "We are not your ordinary travelers. We are here to rescue Vushta!"

"Ah hah!" Emir cried. "I thought as much! Wait a moment! Rescue Vushta from what?"

I wished Emir wouldn't talk so loudly. Others in the street were beginning to stare. Of course, the large number of ferrets around us seemed to be drawing some attention as well. I began to wonder how long we could keep our mission a secret.

"From the Netherhells!" I whispered.

"Oh," Emir replied, a tinge of disappointment in his voice. "You're evangelists, then. I'm afraid it's useless. Vushta has been going to the Netherhells for years!"

"No! You don't understand! Vushta has been taken captive by the Netherhells!"

Emir looked at me as if I had told him the sun always rises at midnight. "No, it couldn't be. Are you still kidding me? Vushta is so full of jokers. Captured by the Netherhells?" He glanced aloft at the gloom that reached to the upper recesses of the cave. "Well, come to think of it, it has been a little dark around here lately."

"Doom!" Hendrek interjected. "You mean you failed to see that Vushta has been taken over by demons?"

"Well," Emir said defensively, "what's so odd about that? A lot of stranger things take place in Vushta every day, let me tell you!"

"Doom," Hendrek repeated.

"Indeed," I remarked. Rescuing Vushta might be more difficult than I had thought. Perhaps it would be best to contact some of the local wizardry. "Do you think you might be able to take us to someone in charge?"

"Oh, you want to go to the Inner City!" Emir exclaimed, brightening perceptibly. "Ah hah! I thought you brought those ferrets for a reason! You can tell me. You're really a new forbidden delight, traveling incognito!"

Norei stepped forward before I could deny Emir's accusation. "Our mission is of the utmost secrecy!" she said. "We will reveal it to you," she added in a whisper, "when we reach our destination."

"Ah hah!" Emir rubbed his hands together gleefully. "So, when you reach your destination, all will be"— he paused meaningfully—"revealed?"

"Indeed," I said a bit doubtfully.

"Oh, permit me to be your guide!" Emir insisted. "No, no! I will not accept any gold for my services! I consider it an honor to be able to lead you to your"— he paused meaningfully again—"revelation!"

"So why do we tarry?" Norei demanded.

"Speak and I shall obey!" Emir responded. "All of you! Follow me to the Inner City!"

And so we began our walk through the streets of Vushta. And what streets they were! I had thought I had seen colors before, but other fabrics and paints and building stones, even people themselves, all were but pale imitations of the true colors of Vushta. I had thought I had heard sounds before, but no music had ever sounded so sweet as that we heard in passing from open windows high above and no laughter ever sounded so inviting as that which drifted from side streets as we walked.

The streets themselves were narrow and crowded for the most part, full of little stalls with people selling everything imaginable, and some things beyond imagining. Not so different, I supposed, from the never-ending Netherhells mall, except that the spirit here was the complete opposite. Back in the Netherhells, you were somehow impelled by useless music to buy useless things for useless places. Here, though, it was different. If you spent your money in Vushta, you were buying life!

And there were women here, also! I had thought I had seen women before, but—well, in this, even my powers of description fail me!

My companions had fallen silent as we walked. The others in our party seemed as overwhelmed as I. Only the Dealer of Death was constantly on the move, jogging from one side of our little group to the other, looking high and low, his every muscle alert—ready, I imagined, for any sudden danger that might confront us.

The Dealer moved with the grace of a panther up to the front of the line. Emir looked at him curiously.

"Pardon me," he said mildly, "but might I ask you a question?"

"Of course!" Emir enthused. "I will be glad to be of any service whatsoever! One hand washes the other, if you catch my"— he paused significantly—"meaning."

"Oh." The Dealer flexed his massive shoulders. "I was wondering—er—if you might know the whereabouts of any—um—wild pigs?"

"Wild pigs?" Emir appeared to be getting truly excited. "Both ferrets and wild pigs? This is much better than I ever imagined!" The portly man winked in the Dealer's direction. "You can find anything in Vushta if you look long enough. But why am I telling you this?" He paused meaningfully. "You should be the one telling me!"

"Doom!"

We stopped in our tracks at Hendrek's cry. The vast warrior's arm shook as he pointed with his cursed warclub to a sign directly ahead.

The place before us looked as if it had been dropped here from somewhere else, certainly someplace other than Vushta. Instead of the customary Vushtan building materials of bright stone or brick, this structure was made of something dark and shiny, some metal perhaps. Instead of having an open front like all the other stalls in the street, this building was enclosed, with a large, brightly lit window to entice you within. I thought

I heard faint but compelling music emanating from somewhere nearby.

"So now do you believe our story?" Norei demanded of Emir.

The portly man stared dumbly at the large sign before us, carved in letters three feet high:

### SLIME-O-RAMA!
*Home of the Famous Slime Burger!*

"I know this all fits in somehow." Emir frowned. "Ferrets and wild pigs *and* Slime Burgers? I *had* noticed this new group of establishments appearing all over town. Good heavens! We *have* been invaded by the Netherhells!"

"At last!" Snarks sighed. "I should have realized that this whole thing was going to be more difficult than I thought. I forgot that, when we went to rescue Vushta, we would be forced to deal with humans!"

Emir shrugged. "Well, it's a natural mistake. I mean, so we've been captured by the Netherhells! There's so much going on in Vushta, who would notice the difference?"

"Indeed," I replied. "So now will you get us to the Inner City with all speed?"

"With all speed!" Emir declared. Before he turned to lead us on, he added, a twinge of disappointment in his voice: "Does this mean you're really not a forbidden delight?"

"I'm afraid not," I admitted.

"Have you thought about going into that line of work?" Emir asked hopefully. "Let me tell you, you have all the ingredients for a real success!"

"We don't have time for that now!" Norei exclaimed. "We must rescue Vushta!"

"Oh, yes." Emir turned with some reluctance. "Rescuing Vushta. Well, I suppose, if it has to be done."

He led us on through the teeming streets.

"Hold!" the Dealer of Death cried a moment later.

"I hear something ahead!"

We paused, but all I could hear were the noises of the ongoing bazaar surrounding us.

"It is still some distance away." The Dealer flexed his ears. "Let us move cautiously."

Norei glanced at me questioningly. I nodded to her and told the Dealer to take the lead. His assassination-trained senses might mean the difference between success and capture by the forces of the Netherhells.

As we moved, I began to hear the noises, too. It was a low sound at first, as if some great beast rumbled beneath the earth. But we were already beneath the earth! What other horrors might there be even farther underground?

But there was another noise as well, some magically amplified voice calling out and an entire crowd of voices responding. I wondered if we should avoid this situation altogether and ask Emir if there was a somewhat more circuitous route into the Inner City. Still, we owed it to ourselves to check the origins of this commotion. Who knew? Perhaps it was created by the very leaders of Vushta I sought!

We turned a corner in the winding street and the sound became suddenly clearer. I could now make out every word the amplified voice was saying:

> We can do just what we please,
> For humans will be on their knees!

And the crowd replied: "Guxx! Guxx! Guxx! Guxx!"

"Doom," Hendrek intoned. "We have found Guxx Unfufadoo."

Apparently we had. I urged the other members of our group to caution. While we had located Guxx, I did not yet wish Guxx to locate us.

We moved quickly but quietly through the crowd, which rapidly shifted from being almost all human to almost all demon. Some of the sickly-looking fiends were carrying signs. A chill ran through my entire being as I read one of the placards:

GUXX UNFUFADOO FOR
SUPREME DICTATOR OF THE WORLD!

We had apparently stumbled upon some sort of political rally. All the other placards the demons carried seemed to be in much the same vein, although some of them said simpler things like "Guxx is the Greatest!" and "Let Guxx Dictate!"

"Brax!" I whispered. "Snarks! Do you know anything about this?"

Brax whistled from behind his cigar. "I knew Guxx was a marketing genius, but this is the big time. He captures the most important city from the surface, he's about to rule the surface world as well, and he uses that one-two punch to corner the highest elected office in all the Netherhells! What master planning!" An involuntary shiver coursed through the demon's frame. "Thank vileness he never sold used weapons!"

"Oh, no," Snarks moaned, close to my side. "This is worse than I thought."

He pointed ahead of us, across the crowd. There, on a raised platform, stood Guxx Unfufadoo in his full ugliness, clothed in a robe of muddy brown, black, gray, and livid purple.

"What is he wearing?" I whispered.

"Oh," Snarks said dismissively. "Those are just the Netherhells colors. I mean that thing behind him!"

I looked beyond Guxx and his platform to a huge, shining structure made of some gray metal. The low, rumbling sound was louder here. It seemed to originate from the structure.

"What is it?" I asked urgently.

"It is a slimeworks," Snarks replied grimly.

"A slimeworks?" I swallowed although my mouth was dry. "What do they do in a slimeworks?"

"You do not wish to know," Snarks said even more grimly than before. "Only now do I realize how serious Guxx really is. If we do not act quickly, the surface world is doomed to a future filled with Slime Burgers!"

There was a commotion on the stage. Some of Guxx Unfufadoo's followers had clambered up to be closer to their hero. Guxx had rapidly retreated and had to be coaxed back to the front of the stage by his aides, who said things like "Don't worry, it isn't her," and "There isn't an old lady within miles of here!" in extremely soothing tones.

Guxx stepped to the edge of the stage again and smiled, the very picture of demonic confidence. He began to speak again.

> Now it is my honor and the time
> To dedicate this edifice to slime!

The demonic audience cheered mightily and waved their placards.

"See what I mean?" Snarks complained. "Oh, why did I let Ebenezum talk me into this? Being banished from the surface world is better than the slimeworks. Maybe I could have learned to like living in the upper air!"

"You should be ashamed of yourself!" Brax rejoined. "And you call yourself a demon! Giving up so easily when there is so much to regain! Don't you remember the Netherhells of yesterday, where a demon was a demon and a slimepit was a pit of slime? Remember going out on vacation to laugh and make fun of the doomed souls? Remember taking your first drink of hot magma and really burning the roof of your mouth? Remember how, the first time you ate Sweet Demon Pie, you got too many brambles in your mouth and they hooked your lips together? Oh, I know, such memories of yesterday are sweet! But the Netherhells can be like that again! They can be a place where a demon was proud to be a used weapons dealer!"

Brax paused, overcome with emotion. "I think it is time for another inspirational cheer."

> I know a place, and it sure is swell,
> The hot, foul, and dirty Netherhells!

He wiped away a tear. "The Netherhells forever!"

"Wait!" The Dealer of Death spoke urgently. "There is something else!"

Again we paused and listened. Perhaps, I hoped wildly, this might be whatever the mighty Guxx was so afraid of. But again I heard nothing but the noises immediately around me: the chanting of the crowd; the political rhymes of Guxx Unfufadoo; the deep rumble of the slimeworks.

"It is behind us!" the Dealer said.

I heard it then. It was the sound of marching feet, and three voices, calling as one:

"We come to collect!"

I had forgotten all about the Dread Collectors! What a time for them to catch up to us, with our quarry almost within our grasp! Whatever we did, we could not let them catch us!

"Doom," Hendrek intoned, echoing my sentiments. "What do we do now?"

"There is only one way to go," the Dealer of Death remarked. "Toward our quarry." And with that he began to run full speed toward the slimeworks.

"He's right!" Norei agreed.

"Doom!" Hendrek chimed in.

"Revitalization!" Zzzzz rejoined.

"The Netherhells forever!" Brax exclaimed.

"Eep! Eep eep! Eep eep eep!" the ferrets chorused.

"Oh, why am I doing this?" Snarks yelped.

"Excuse me, but I have pressing business elsewhere," Emir muttered.

All but Emir began to run through the demonic crowd. What else could I do but join them?

# FIFTEEN

*There is the truth, and there are lies, and there is nothing on Earth or in the Netherhells that does not fall under one of these two headings, with the exception of politics.*

—*from* The Teachings of Ebenezum,
*Volume LXXXVIII*

I drew my sword as I ran.

"Not again!" Cuthbert wailed. "Oh! Watch out! There are demons everywhere!"

"We will collect you for Guxx!" The Collectors' voices reverberated above the crowd. They seemed much closer than before. The demons were milling around in confusion. I pushed a placard roughly out of the way and muscled my way through the crowd with all speed. I couldn't let the Collectors get me!

"We will catch you with our claws!" the Dread Collectors said in unison.

"Oh, no!" Cuthbert moaned. "Not them! Not more ichor!"

A gaggle of demons, surprised by the talking sword, leaped out of the way. I found my path clear for a dozen paces. Perhaps Cuthbert had his uses after all.

"Listen," the sword said in a more confidential tone. "Have you ever thought of other ways I might be employed? I have many fine uses besides fighting, you know. Not only am I good at magical communication over great distances and glowing in the dark, but I am excellent at cutting cheese!"

I booted aside a small green demon who had had the misfortune to wander in my path, then swung my sword above my head as with as much menace as possible. Another dozen demons scattered before me.

"Yes," Cuthbert continued, "I'm actually capable of over one hundred and one common household uses, but does anyone ever think of me that way? No, sir! It's always Cuthbert, slash this, Cuthbert, hack that!"

A loud voice boomed over the crowd:

> Who are these interlopers who toward me plow?
> Stop them, my followers! Stop them now!

So Guxx had noticed us at last.

"So it's the really big demon!" the Dealer of Death cried. "I lost you when we fell into the Netherhells! Now, though, I get another try!"

The Dealer glanced at me, all boyish enthusiasm. "I know that demons squish, but I've never been able to strangle a really big one! Who needs a wild pig? Maybe this rhyming fellow can squish enough to be really satisfying!" He turned and ran for Guxx's platform, clearing clumps of demons with every bound.

Guxx screamed again to his followers:

> We are many! Together we stand!
> We must drive these invaders from our land!

"Doom!" Hendrek swung his enchanted warclub before him, dispensing with a dozen demons at every blow. Those too fast for the warrior's club ran in any direction they could save for the one in which we were going. The path between us and the platform was clearing rapidly.

I detected a note of panic in Guxx's next rhyme:

> Oh, supporters, I am on my knees!
> Protect your dictator elect! Please?

"Quickly now!" Norei called to the rest of our little band. "We have them on the run! Now the attack truly begins!" Her hands flew through a half dozen quick conjures. Small buckets of water appeared above what few demons still barred our way. Two dozen wet demons screamed and fled. There was no one between Guxx and our force now. Nothing could stop us!

"Have no fear!" three voices called from much too close. "We will collect them all!"

"Can't you humans move?" Snarks screamed in terror. "They're gaining on us!" He ran past me, followed closely by Brax and Zzzzz. I never knew demons could move so fast.

"This is the one who escaped!" three voices shouted seemingly in my ear. "We will collect him now! We will give him to Guxx!"

No! I was too close to fail now! I would confront their leader with Ebenezum's spell! Then I would be safe from the Dread Collectors forever!

But there were other complications as well. The demonic hordes had become aware of the Collectors' presence and had paused in their flight. It was only a matter of seconds before they turned around and joined the attack.

I reached the steps that led up to the platform. The Dealer had already climbed to the top and Hendrek was in close pursuit. Our demon allies ringed the bottom of the stairs, each holding whatever weapon they had managed to find. Snarks still carried the metal pole he had found in the decimated shop and Zzzzz had grabbed hold of a sharp-edged placard. Brax had redrawn his dagger, while in the other hand he held his lit cigar. I knew they would hold off our enemies for as long as they could. If Guxx Unfufadoo were triumphant this day, it meant the end of their way of life.

The three demons were, of course, surrounded by an army of bright-eyed ferrets.

"Oh, no!" Cuthbert shrieked. "We're in for it now!"

With a blood-curdling yell, the demonic hordes ran toward us, the Dread Collectors at their front, all claws and fangs and fury, moving with unbelievable speed.

"We will collect!" the monsters bellowed.

I glanced at Norei, still by my side. If we were going to die, at least we would die together!

"To the platform!" we cried as one and quickly ran up the stairs. I held Cuthbert aloft, ready for any attack from above. With my free hand, I fished within my shirt for the piece of parchment that held the spell that was the key to our defeat of Guxx Unfufadoo.

All I found were pieces of hat. I cursed my luck. It must have fallen in with the remains of my earlier aborted attempts at magic. Unless—oh, of course! How foolish of me! This shirt had a pocket.

Norei and I reached the top of the platform to see Guxx Unfufadoo and the Dealer of Death but a few paces apart. The Dealer would take a step forward and Guxx would take a step back. This drama would not last long. The large demon was very close to the platform's edge.

Guxx shouted as he backed away.

> I have ripped the heart from many of man
> When I have fought them hand to hand!

"Then why do you run?" The Dealer smiled. "You have nothing to fear from me, or so you say. After all, I only want to feel how your neck squishes."

"Doom!" Hendrek called. "Be careful! His strength grows with every rhyme he makes!"

Of course! That must be the fiend's foul strategy! He would keep the Dealer at bay until he had rhymed so much that he was practically unstoppable!

"Hold, Dealer!" Norei shouted from where she stood by my side. "Wuntvor has a spell from Ebenezum, guaranteed to keep Guxx at bay!"

I nodded grimly and walked across the platform until I stood by the Dealer's side, Cuthbert the sword still in my right hand, ready for any treachery on the part of Guxx.

"You don't scare me with your talk of spells!" Guxx retorted. "For I will send you straight to . . ." The demon paused and shook his foul head. "No. That doesn't work. You're already there! Let's try this one: You don't scare me with your sorcery, for I can stop you with my force—er—that one isn't very good either, is it?"

"Don't worry!" Snarks yelled encouragingly. "He's nothing without his speechwriters!"

We had Guxx now! Without his rhymes, he could not increase his strength and the Dealer could defeat him easily. I reached into my pocket in triumph, ready to deal the final blow to this would-be demonic dictator.

But my pocket was empty.

Where was the parchment?

I had a sudden, clear vision of a small red card and another small, white piece of parchment fluttering to the ground in a dungeon many miles away. A troll had picked up the card. I knew now what had been on the piece of paper.

"Wait! I've got it!" Guxx Unfufadoo cleared his demonic throat.

> You don't scare me with your magic
> And now your end will be very tragic!

Guxx grinned in triumph.

"Let me take him!" the Dealer growled. He leaped forward, but Guxx pushed him back with a flick of demonic claws. The demon had become too powerful!

"Wuntvor!" Norei said. "Your spell?"

Still holding my sword aloft as inadequate protection against the advancing demon, I glanced at my beloved. How could I tell her that I had lost the only spell that would save us?

"Oh, no!" Cuthbert moaned. "Can't we talk this over?"

Guxx Unfufadoo smiled as he bore down upon me.

"Now I'll defeat you! The Netherhells knows, for with every rhyme my great strength—ferrets?"

Yes, once again my army of ferrets had come to the

rescue! With a great chorus of *eeps*, they leaped upon the advancing demon.

"Norei!" I cried. "The spell is gone!"

"Watch out!" Snarks called from below. "The Collectors!"

"Doom!" Hendrek remarked.

"Revitalize everything!" Zzzzz added.

"What can we do?" Norei shouted.

The Dread Collectors' attack had forced our demonic allies to retreat to the platform. Now the Collectors were climbing the stairs with amazing speed.

"There's only one thing to do!" Cuthbert screamed. "Run!"

For once, Cuthbert was right.

"But where can we go!?" Norei asked.

Guxx had shaken off the ferrets as a dog might shake off rainwater. He stepped toward us again.

"We will collect you now." The Collectors were almost to the top of the stairs.

The platform was far too high. If we jumped, it would be to our deaths.

I looked around rapidly and saw a silver door at the rear of the platform that apparently led into the building beyond.

"We must go through there!" I pointed. "Into the slimeworks!"

"Doom!" Hendrek said as he followed us in.

# SIXTEEN

Ebenezum: *There are a number of ways of dealing with extreme stress. For example, when all about you is going wrong and it looks as if you might not survive your current circumstances, it is often helpful to think of a pleasant thought.*

Interviewer: *Do you mean, for example, how good it will feel to strangle, pummel, and utterly destroy my enemy?*

Ebenezum: *Well, no, you do not quite have the spirit of it. Think rather of a flower, or rather, a group of flowers. Picture bright yellow daisies, perhaps, or stately red roses, full and fragrant. And now that you have this thought in your mind, think how lovely those flowers will look on the grave of your enemy once he has been strangled, pummeled, and utterly destroyed. It is only in this way that the besieged wizard may find inner peace.*

—from Conversations with Ebenezum;
A Series of Dialogues with the Greatest Wizard
in the Western Kingdoms,
*fourth edition*

"My mother didn't raise me to go into a slimeworks," Snarks said behind me.

"Quiet!" I demanded. "We have to keep our wits about us! It is the only way we can escape!"

I led the others quickly through the dimly lit corridor we had found at the other side of the door. There was barely enough light to see. Still, I was reluctant to use Cuthbert's glowing ability. After all, I could think of no better beacon than a shining sword to guide our enemies to us.

I have mentioned that I heard a low rumble as I approached this great gleaming building. Now that we were within the structure, I no longer so much heard the rumbling as felt it beneath my feet with every step I took. I thought about asking Snarks about the nature of the noise, but was afraid of the answer I would get.

I still held Cuthbert before me, in case of another demonic attack. Norei was immediately to my rear, then Hendrek and the Dealer, followed by our three demonic cohorts. I thought I also heard another noise beneath the rumbling, like dozens of tiny feet scrambling against metal. So perhaps some of my ferrets were with us as well! It was astonishing how quickly I had become attached to the little creatures. But then again, in a certain way, I was responsible for every single one of them!

"Ouch!" Cuthbert cried. "Watch it there!"

I seemed to have bumped my sword against a door.

"Hold!" I said quietly to those behind me. I pushed at the door. It swung away easily.

"We are going through," I told the others. "Keep together and keep quiet. There's no telling what's out there!"

"I know what's out—" Snarks began.

"Quiet!" I repeated. "There will be time enough for talk once we get out of this place!" And I stepped through a door onto another platform.

Voices drifted up to me from far below.

"And this is where we make our special sauce!"

I looked down. The platform we had stepped out on overlooked a huge room filled with enormous vats. All the vats appeared to be filled with liquid, gray and bubbling. In one corner of the room stood a group of demons gazing in wonder at the process before them. It was from this group that the voices drifted.

"We here at Slime-O-Rama are very proud of our sauces!" said a demon who faced all the others. "Our special sauce has made Slime Burgers what they are today!''

The huge gray vats continued to bubble and belch. As long as we kept our voices low, for the moment we were safe from detection.

"What's going on?" Norei whispered.

"It's a guided tour of the new slimeworks," Snarks interjected. "It's part of something they call the Slime-O-Rama Outreach Program. When I was in school, they used to bring us to a slimeworks every year." Snarks shivered. "I still remember their slogan: 'Helping hands through slime!' "

"Then you know the design of such a building?" I asked, the excitement causing me to speak more loudly than I should. I glanced nervously down at the demons in the other corner of the room, but they still seemed busily involved in a discussion of the vatting process. I continued in a whisper:

"You can tell us what everything is! And you can find us a way out of here!"

"Unfortunately," Snarks replied, "I know everything that goes on within these walls far too well. 'We are now in the boiling room, where the liquid slime is boiled down to its proper gooey, stick-to-the ribs quality that Slime Burger lovers love to eat!' I can repeat every word they're saying down there!"

"Yes," Norei urged, "but can you find a way out of here?"

Snarks considered her question. "The fact that they are conducting guided tours gives us a slight chance. Perhaps we can disguise ourselves as tourists and get past the guards. If that doesn't work, there's only one way we're getting out of here!"

"And how is that?" I prompted.

Snarks pointed down at the vats. "As slime."

"Doom," Hendrek said. "We leave as slime?"

Snarks nodded his small, green head. "That's the thing about slime. No matter what you put into it

—mud, demons, humans—it still comes out slime.''

"Doom," Hendrek repeated.

But I could not believe we did not have a chance. There had to be other ways to escape, and ways to get at Guxx as well, if only we could think of them. My master had said that I was gifted with luck. If I ever needed that gift, it was now!

I turned to my beloved. "Norei. Misfortune has caused me to lose the spell that would have enabled us to capture one of Guxx's nose hairs. But you are a full-fledged witch. Surely you know some spell we can use."

"Oh, dear," she replied, frowning. "That may be something of a problem. We lived on a farm, you know. I can perform a great deal of household magic, and I know more than a few crop spells, plus a few specialized things I memorized before I left home to meet you. But I'm afraid, throughout my magical training, as much as I would like to tell you otherwise, I have had very little dealing with nose hair."

Oh, how I hated to see my beloved frown so! "Do not worry!" I said. " 'Tis only my desperation that made me ask such a thing of you! We will just have to find some other means to succeed."

Norei looked thoughtful. "Still, Wuntvor, I may be able to come up with something."

There was a substantial commotion behind us. I hoped for one mad instant that it was only the ferrets. But I knew, as I heard their cheerful *eeps* all around, that it had to be something far worse.

Four words reverberated down the metal corridor through which we had escaped.

"We come to collect!"

"This is getting a little tiresome," Snarks commented. "Couldn't those guys come up with something else?"

"Maybe we can sell them some new material," Brax suggested. "I think it may be time I got out of the used weapons business."

"I think it may be time we got out of the Netherhells altogether," Snarks replied.

A set of Collector claws sheared through the door behind us.

"There is one consolation," the Dealer of Death remarked softly. "I will have a second opportunity to find if these creatures have necks." He smiled grimly. "Or I shall die trying."

"We come to destroy!" the Collectors cried as one.

"Now see," Snarks mused. "They used a new word. That at least shows a little originality. Maybe these monsters don't have to be totally boring after all."

"We come to maim!" the Collectors screamed. "To torture! To kill!" Claws shredded what little was left of the door and the entranceway around it.

"You know," Snarks said, "I think an awful lot of this is done just for effect."

"We've got to get out of here!" Cuthbert insisted. And again the sword was right.

There was a set of narrow stairs that wound down between the vats. I raised Cuthbert in the air and yelled for the others to follow me.

I walked quickly but carefully down the stone stairs. Every third step seemed to hold a puddle of slime, and it would do no good to slip and fall now. We needed all our wits about us if we were to have any chance of success.

A railing began where the steps curled around one of the vats. I put my hand on it to give me stability, but pulled it away as soon as I touched its wet, gooey surface. I absently sniffed my fingers. It was slime all right.

I was reminded of the thick gray sludge between two pieces of bread I was offered as part of my dungeon torment. This is what the demons were doing to Vushta! And they would bring Slime-O-Rama to the surface world as well if we failed in our task. I had a clear, horrifying vision of Wizard's Woods, where I was born and raised, entirely covered by slime.

While I was alive, that would not happen!

I could no longer hear demonic voices on the floor below us. The tour must have moved on to the next room. That meant one complication at least was out of the way. Now all we had to do was lose the Dread Collectors, somehow temporarily immobilize Guxx Unfufadoo long enough to prune a nose hair, and escape back to the surface world without being caught. I swallowed again, though I did not remember having any saliva in my mouth since I had entered the Netherhells. We would have to face each of our problems as we came to them.

The gloom was far deeper between the vats. I asked Cuthbert to give me a little light. The sword obliged with hardly any comment. I pointed it down to guide me to the floor.

"Glurph!" the sword exclaimed.

In Cuthbert's light, I could see I had reached the bottom of the steps, except that, instead of dry floor beneath me, there was a layer of slime.

I lifted Cuthbert's point out of the gray muck.

"I thought there was nothing worse than ichor!" the sword wailed. "I was wrong!"

How deep was the slime? Could we still walk out of here or would we have to swim? There was only one way to find out. I planted my feet on the last step above the liquid.

"Have you no compassion?" Cuthbert protested as I immersed it once again in slime.

The sword submerged only halfway before I hit something solid.

"Quickly!" I called to the others. "There's a layer of slime on the floor that will slow us down. Get off the stairs as fast as you can!"

With that, I jumped to the ground. My feet oozed downwards in slime. And I heard an all-too-familiar voice from the platform above.

Get them, Collectors, for they are mine!
Don't let them escape through the slime!

"We will collect for Guxx!" the Collectors screamed
as they rushed down the steps.

The other members of my band splashed down
around me. I walked on as best as I could, intent on getting as far away from the Collectors as possible. It was
rather like walking through soup, except that the smell
that rose about us made me think that perhaps the soup
was a few days too old. I had to be careful to plant my
feet firmly every time I took a step, or I might slip entirely below the gray muck.

"Doo—oof!" Others in my party seemed to be having similar problems. Hendrek picked himself back up,
his body now half-covered with slime.

"Snarks!" I called. "Come up here with me. Which
is the best way to go?" Even as I spoke, though, I was
still moving. I saw a large archway ahead filled with
light. Noise seemed to come from there as well. Until
Snarks told me otherwise, I decided that arch was our
destination. Whatever lay beyond had to be better than
slime.

I risked a look above us. Guxx still watched from his
vantage point atop the platform, but the Collectors,
with their horrible speed, were already over halfway
down the stairs. I did my best to redouble my pace.

Snarks was saying something as he swam up to meet
me, but it was lost in the growing noise that emanated
from the archway ahead. I could make out some sort of
voices; chanting perhaps, or periodic yells or cheers. It
was hard to tell more than that because of the other
noise that came from there as well, a steady roaring
sound that grew louder with every step, underlaid with a
rhythmic crunching noise. There was an odd familiar-
ity about that crunching, until I realized that its rhythms
were the same as the rumbling sound I had heard even
before we had entered this building. We would finally

get to see what would make such a colossal noise.

Something pulled at my sleeve. I turned to see Snarks looking more frightened than he had ever before.

"No!" The truth-telling demon shrieked over the noise. "We don't want to go in there."

I tried to explain that we had to. The Collectors were almost on top of us. If we turned around, they would catch us for sure.

"No, you don't understand!" Snarks insisted. "We don't dare go in there! That's the grinding room."

The grinding room? I stopped my forward flight and paused to listen more carefully to the sounds coming from the room ahead. Perhaps those voices weren't chanting, or even yelling. In fact, the closer I got to it, the more it sounded like screaming.

"We collect you now!" I spun about to see all three Dread Collectors reaching the foot of the stairs. What could we do? There was no place for us to go!

And then the Collectors leaped into the slime.

"Get out of their way!" Norei yelled as they slid toward us. My beloved had spotted their weakness! In their eagerness to collect us, the monsters had entered the slime at full speed. Now there was no way for them to stop.

I pulled Snarks up close against one of the vats. The three Collectors sped past us, all sliding uncontrollably on the slime.

"We have gone too far!" all three cried as they slid beyond us into the grinding room.

It was then that I really heard the screams. I wondered if it were the Dread Collectors making the noise, or other things in that grinding room that were waiting to be ground. Whatever it was, I had no wish to investigate it further. With the Collectors out of our way, perhaps there was some way we could overpower Guxx.

"Turn around!" I called to the others. "Back up the stairs!"

The rest of my party eagerly complied.

"Dealer!" I shouted. "Hendrek! We must detain Guxx!"

"My pleasure," the Dealer responded, leaping up the stairs four at a time.

"Doom," Hendrek remarked as he rapidly lumbered behind.

Guxx raged overhead:

> You try to capture me, you dunces!
> Well, I'll no longer pull my punches!

"Dunces and punches?" Snarks called from by my side. "Do you call that a rhyme?"

Guxx growled, even more furious than before.

"Now you question my rhyming talent!

"Well, I will throw you off this planet—er—no, I know that one doesn't work either. See here, you've got me upset. I can never rhyme properly when I'm upset." The fearsome demon leader pointed at Snarks. "I know who you are! I knew there was a reason we banished you. Just wait a minute while I get my strength back. Let's see . . ."

> Now you question my rhyming skill.
> Well, I know someone I can—urracht!

The Dealer had lauched himself straight for Guxx Unfufadoo's neck. Guxx still had enough strength to at least partially break away and draw a ragged breath. The two of them rolled about on the platform above us.

"Quickly!" I said to the others. "We must join them as well!"

"Watch your step!" Cuthbert called as I hurried up the stairs. "Say, I tell you what. How about I keep giving you this nice, modulated light, and we can watch the others beat up that big demon thing? Doesn't that sound like a good idea?"

I did not bother to answer. Instead, I called to Norei, who had already climbed halfway up the stairs.

"Have you thought of any spells?"

"I'll come up with something!" she called back. "I only have to think what demons and farming have in common!"

The commotion became even louder above us.

"Now I have it! I've broken free!" Guxx screamed overhead. "Now we'll see who the winner will—urk!"

The demon leader had temporarily bested the Dealer of Death, but he had forgotten completely about Hendrek, who had managed to connect with a vicious blow of the doomed club Headbasher.

"Who? What?" Guxx queried, temporarily under the dread Headbasher's fearsome spell. "Oh, that's right. I'm Guxx Unfufadoo, soon to be the Supreme Ruler of Everything!" His senses once again about him, the demon deflected a second blow with a well-placed set of claws.

Norei was on the platform now. Her hands flew as she uttered a quick spell. A cloud appeared immediately above Guxx and almost as immediately let loose with a torrent of water.

Guxx glared at her, somewhat dampened but otherwise unfazed.

> You try to stop the mighty Guxx with water.
> But from my task I shall not falter!

I reached the platform then, with Snarks hot on my heels.

"Grab him now!" Snarks cried. "He can't possibly be gaining any strength with rhymes like that!"

The Dealer approached Guxx, more cautiously this time, but with no easing of his deadly purpose. Perhaps, I thought, we really could subdue Guxx this time!

And then three voices called from down below:

"We are back from the grinding room!"

Oh, no! The Dread Collectors had somehow survived. Even now I could hear them coming up the stairs.

Guxx laughed evilly.

"Now we will kill you all!" he shouted and launched into another rhyme:

> While it may not yet be June,
> You will never see the moon,
> For it is your death I croon,
> And we will eat you with a spoon!

The Dealer of Death attacked Guxx then, but it was already too late. The demon leader pushed the Dealer aside with a flick of his claws. He laughed again.

"We have you now!" he yelled. "The old rhyme schemes are always the best!"

So we would die now. There appeared to be no other choice. I turned to the edge of the stairway. I would face the rapidly climbing Collectors, sword in hand. Perhaps I could at least wound one before my demise.

"What are you doing?" my sword shrieked.

I calmly outlined my death plan.

"But couldn't you do something else?" Cuthbert begged.

And then I realized, of course I could! Cuthbert was not my only weapon. And this time I still had Wonk, the horn of persuasion, tied to my belt!

I quickly undid the sack as the Collectors reached the platform's edge.

"We collect you no—" they began.

I put Wonk to my lips and blew.

The Collectors froze in their tracks. I moved toward them, still blowing relentlessly. The monsters looked about wildly, seeking some means of escape. But I had stepped around them and now stood between them and the stairs.

The three Dread Collectors looked at each other for a single instant, then jumped as one off the platform.

"We are slime!" they screamed in unison. And they plunged into the vats below.

I looked to those of us remaining on the platform.

Everyone, Guxx included, was cowering where they stood, ears covered.

Norei came over and leaned heavily against me. She looked deep into my eyes.

"Wuntvor?" she whispered. "Could you do one thing for me?"

"Anything, my beloved!" I replied.

She smiled sweetly. "Unless you absolutely have to, promise me you'll never blow that thing again."

"Indeed," I agreed. "Let us see if we can get what we need from Guxx!"

"Thank the Netherhells you stopped!" Snarks moaned. "Another moment of that noise and I would have opted for slime as well!"

"Come," I said. "We must take Guxx now!"

# SEVENTEEN

*Wizards should not go seeking revenge, killing, or death in general. After all, revenge, killing, and death in general have a way of showing up whether you are looking for them or not.*

—*from* The Teachings of Ebenezum,
*Volume I*

Guxx Unfufadoo staggered to his feet as we approached. He shook his head and frowned with pain. All his fangs showed when he grimaced. His voice shook as he spoke.

You think to beat me with the horn,
But you shall soon be tossed and—

I blew Wonk again, only a short blast this time, but it was enough to drive Guxx to his knees.

"I thought I asked you not to do that again!" Norei cried from my side. She appeared to have fallen to her knees as well.

"Indeed," I replied. "It could not be helped. If we can get a nose hair, I will never have to do it again." With my free hand, I drew forth Cuthbert.

"What do you want now?" the sword shrieked.

"Don't worry," I said reassuringly. "You won't have to kill anyone this time."

"Oh, thank goodness!" the sword exclaimed, greatly relieved. "There's been too much happening lately. My nerves are all on edge!"

"This will all be over soon," I assured the sword. "All we have to do is cut out a single one of this demon's nose hairs."

"You want me to go in there?" Cuthbert screeched.
"Inside a demon's nose? Have you no code of honor?"

"Come on now!" I chided. "It won't be so bad. A
single snip and you're done."

"That's easy for you to say!" the sword complained.
"You don't have to go into some strange creature's
orifice! Heavens knows where it's been!"

I could see this was going to be more difficult than I
had expected. And, realistically, Cuthbert had a point.
He was a fairly broad sword and, as large as Guxx was,
his nose wasn't really huge. It would be a delicate opera-
tion at best. There had to be a better way.

Guxx began to stir again.

"A single move," I warned, "and you will hear the
horn."

"Don't move!" everyone urged fervently. "Please
don't move!"

And then I had an idea.

"Norei," I asked, "you say you are most familiar
with household and farming spells?"

"Yes?" she replied.

"Then you could know some simple growth spells!"

"Of course," she answered. "Why?"

"Is it possible to apply one of those spells to a single
nose hair?"

"Oh!" She brightened as she caught my idea. "It
would be simplicity itself!"

She made three small gestures, combined with a short
string of magic phrases. Something black and coarse
poked its way from Guxx's nostril.

"This is a little disgusting," Norei admitted.

"Hey," Snarks retorted. "It's the Netherhells. What
did you expect?"

The hair continued to grow. I waited until a good foot
of it was exposed to the open air.

"All right," I said to Cuthbert. "Now we will cut."

"If we have to," the sword replied as I set to work.
"Ouch! Ooh! Hey boss, this just isn't going to work!"

Cuthbert was right. No matter how I chopped or sliced, it made no dent. Guxx Unfufadoo was a virtually indestructible demon. That meant that his nose hair was indestructible as well!

"You mean there's no way you can cut this?" I said in alarm.

"Sorry," Cuthbert answered. "I may be magic, but I'm not perfect."

A great shout came from deep within the corridor we had used to enter the slimeworks.

"Uh-oh," Snarks said. "It sounds like reinforcements! We have to get out of here!"

"Doom!" Hendrek added. "But what about the hair?"

I had to make a quick decision. "We have to keep the growing spell going! Norei, can you reinforce the spell in any way? Cuthbert, we need to contact my master!"

Guxx laughed from where he sat.

> You will never cut my hair
> And my reinforcments are almost—

His voice died in his throat as I pointed at Wonk. I handed the horn to Norei. "It will work as well in her hands," I warned the demon. "We may not be able to get all of your hair, but at least we'll take one end!"

With that, I swung the sword about my head three times and the magic window opened. It once again showed the great hall of the East Vushta academy and two wizards dressed in red.

"I can see you talking about theory while demons eat you!" Zimplitz said.

"I can see you with your simple, practical spells, totally inadequate for dealing with the Netherhells!" Snorphosio retorted.

"Would you people be quiet!" I shouted.

Snorphosio peered through the window. "Oh, dear. 'Tis the apprentice. We're not always like this, you know. You see us at our worst. It's the stress, I'm sure—"

"I don't care what it is!" I cried. I rapidly outlined our situation. "Is there some way to get us out of here?"

"Certainly," Zimplitz agreed. "A simple retrieval spell."

"Well," Snorphosio added, "I don't know how simple that would be. There are a lot of variables . . ."

The noises from the hallway were getting louder. They seemed to come from a great many very angry demons.

"If it's not simple enough to retrieve us right now," I insisted, "I don't think you'll see us again!"

"Well . . ." Snorphosio began.

"Put your hands together!" Zimplitz directed. "We'll get you out!"

The window disappeared as I placed Cuthbert back in its scabbard. I carefully wrapped a couple of feet of nose hair around my wrist and told all those going with me to join hands. Brax and Zzzzz both politely refused.

"If you can defeat Guxx," Brax added, waving his cigar, "I can go back to my day job. Hendrek, I'll be seeing you soon about a payment!"

"Doom," the warrior replied.

"I can't leave this place now!" Zzzzz responded. "You've given my life new meaning. Revitalization forever!"

With that, the horde of angry demons burst into the room.

Would the magician's spell come too late? I held Norei's hand even tighter than before. Perhaps I could say some final words before the end.

"Norei, I . . . " I began.

But the rest of my words were lost to the wind. A wind that seemed to spring from nowhere, that surrounded us and lifted us aloft, over the platform and vats, then out of the slimeworks. We seemed to be moving at tremendous speed. I caught a single glimpse of the pastel towers of Vushta, then another of the garish colors of the Netherhells mall, then we were plunged into darkness.

The wind ceased. We had returned to light. I blinked. We all sat on the floor of the large hall of the wizards' extension school.

"Is that a spell"—Zimplitz beamed—"or is that a spell?"

I looked about the room. Snorphosio stood by Zimplitz's side, still looking skeptical. The wizards were flanked by their students, plus a couple of newcomers in sorcerous gear.

"Where is Ebenezum?" I asked.

"He is on his way," Zimplitz replied. "You did arrive rather suddenly, after all. In the meantime, the rest of us are ready. Do you have the nose hair?"

I proudly showed them the strand still wrapped around my knuckles. The hair, apparently, had not been broken by Zimplitz's magic. Instead, it stretched out of the hall into the foyer and, I imagined, far beyond that.

"We were unable to cut it," I explained.

Something nuzzled my knee. It was small and covered with slime.

"Eep!"

"Eep eep!"

"Eep eep eep!"

So Zimplitz's spell had rescued the ferrets as well! Well, at least some of the ferrets. I had never had time to pause and make an accurate count.

"Do you mean," Snorphosio's voice cut through my reverie, "that one end of this nose hair is still attached to Guxx Unfufadoo?"

I nodded. " 'Twas the best we could do under the circumstances."

"Men!" Snorphosio cried. "We must be more than ready! We will be attacked at any second!"

The earth began to shake. As dazed as my party was,

we regained our feet. We all realized that this would be the final battle.

The newly refinished floor of the Great Hall burst asunder. A mighty voice cried above the roar:

I can follow my hair wherever it grows.
I will teach humans to pick my nose!

And Guxx appeared in our midst, leading a demon horde!

Demons seemed to be everywhere! I fell back by the line of student wizards, all busily conjuring, thinking their protection would give me a moment to collect myself. But a great purple and green demon appeared from nowhere to sweep them from their feet before they could complete a single spell.

Grimly, I drew Cuthbert from its scabbard.

"Not again!" it began.

"Quiet!" I instructed the sword. "If we lose this battle, you'll be owned by demons!"

The purple and green creature turned to me. It was easily twice my height. I barely ducked beneath its sweeping claws.

"Watch out!" Cuthbert warned.

I had watched the thing's claws, but I had forgotten about its heavily barbed tail! It whistled through the air as it descended to crush my skull. Perhaps it was instinct, or perhaps it was the magic sword actually doing its job for a change, but Cuthbert met the tail as it fell and neatly sliced it in two. The barbs flew away, missing me completely. Dark ichor sprayed from the wound. Cuthbert, to its credit, did nothing but whimper.

The huge creature cried in rage and pain, and spun to attack me again. But a dozen small, slime-covered shapes streaked between us, attaching themselves to various parts of the demon's anatomy. The monster screamed as it fell, thrashing about in a vain attempt to rid itself of ferrets.

My small charges had once again given me a moment

to think. If only I had Wonk to hand, I could rout these demons in an instant. But I had given the horn to Norei. Would she think to use it? I could not see her in the battle. All I could see were demons.

"Doom!"

"Urk!" Hendrek's enchanted warclub, Headbasher, dispatched a demon that had been flying straight for my head.

"Urracchhtt!"

"Urracchhtt!"

The Dealer of Death strode through the room, strangling demons with one hand or the other as he passed.

"Men!" I cried to the two of them. "Forget these other demons! We must take Guxx!"

"Doom," Hendrek said, clubbing his way to my side.

"My pleasure," the Dealer remarked, nonchalantly strangling a demon or two as he walked my way.

I looked quickly about the room. Guxx stood upon the dais, facing Zimplitz. Snorphosio lay in a heap at Guxx's feet.

"I'll drink his blood to slake my thirst!" Guxx cried over the unconscious mage. "He should not have talked. He should conjure first!"

This was worse than I thought. Guxx seemed to be back in prime rhyming form!

But Zimplitz was unabashed. "All right, fiend!" he cried. "Let's see how you deal with practical magic!"

Guxx reached out and flicked Zimplitz from the dais before the mage could complete his mystic gesture!

> Your magic is dead, your end is near,
> There is nothing left for Guxx to—

"Where is that pest!?" An elderly, cracked voice broke through Guxx's rhyme.

"No!" the demon lord screamed. "Not her!"

Using her umbrella for support, a gray-haired old lady pushed herself out of the hole through which the demons had arrived.

"There he is!" she cried in triumph as she waved her umbrella aloft.

"Mother!" Tomm the sorcery student cried.

"Get her, demons!" Guxx shrieked. "Whatever you do, get her!"

The demonic horde leaped for the old lady.

"Mother!"

Tomm and his fellow students followed the horde.

Guxx grinned as he saw the umbrella disappear under a pile of demons.

> I've now gotten rid of one more fool,
> For in this place Netherhells will rule!

The demon lord laughed evilly.

The demon horde was occupied. It was time to confront Guxx.

"The Netherhells will never rule here!" I shouted. "Guxx, you are defeated!"

At a sign from me, the Dealer, Hendrek, and I rushed the dais.

Guxx grabbed Headbasher in one hand and the Dealer's throat in the other. He threw both warriors away as if they were pieces of parchment. He smiled at me as he spoke:

> So this is what you call defeat.
> Victory is not this sweet!

He reached forward to crush my head in his claws.

"No!" I screamed.

A bunch of daisies fell from my shirt. There must be a magical overabundance here. The pieces of magic cap within my shirt were working again.

"No!" I shouted. "Yes! No! Yes! No! Yes!" Thousands of daisies and scarves exploded outward, straight into Guxx's face.

The demon lord screamed with rage.

> You try this demon to distract!
> Now I will kill you! That's a fact!

But not until I had exhausted every weapon in my arsenal! Holding Cuthbert before me for what small protection the sword still afforded me, I took a deep breath.

"Perhaps!" I cried. "Perhaps! Perhaps! Perhaps! Perhaps! Perhaps!"

Guxx was attacked by a legion of ferrets.

The demon lord tossed every single one aside.

> Now at last we are all alone.
> I'll drink your blood and crunch your bones!

Guxx Unfufadoo grinned broadly as he approached.

There was a crash. The hall's huge oak door had been pushed open by some colossal force.

"Indeed," a deep voice rumbled behind me.

It was my master, Ebenezum, greatest wizard in all the Western Kingdoms!

Guxx's smile faltered as he looked beyond me to the mage.

> I have defeated you once before—
> I will gladly oblige if you want some more!

Ebenezum raised his hands. A mighty wind sprang up, pushing Guxx against the dais.

"Wuntvor?" my master asked calmly. "Do you have the nose hair?"

"Yes!" I answered. One end was still wrapped around my knuckles.

"If I might have it?" the wizard requested.

I unwrapped the strand from about my hand and passed it to my master.

"Guxx is immune to any magic!" the demon cried as he struggled to rise from the dais. "Try it and your end is tragic!"

"Indeed," my master replied. "I think not."

He took one end of the demon's nose hair and lifted it to his own nostril. And then the wizard sneezed.

Guxx laughed hideously.

You sneeze at magic no matter what you do!
And now Guxx will use his claws—wahhhchooo!

And Guxx began to sneeze as well.

My master quickly blew his nose on what looked to be a new set of robes and said a quick series of spells. Guxx's sneezes doubled and redoubled.

"No!" The demon sneezed. "I am not—" Guxx sneezed again. "I will rhyme—" And sneezed again. "Well, perhaps maybe I am—"

My master intoned another group of mystic words. Guxx seemed about to sneeze, but breathed in instead. He seemed about to sneeze again, but inhaled some more. A look of panic came over his countenance.

Ebenezum snapped his fingers. The room was filled with a mighty roar.

When the dust had cleared, there was a hole where the demon lord had stood. Guxx Unfufadoo appeared to have sneezed himself back down to the Netherhells. Demons screamed in terror and leaped into the hole to follow their leader.

Dragonfire came through the windows to singe what few fiends remained. They quickly ran to join the others.

"Master?" I called.

"Indeed," the mage reflected. "Guxx Unfufadoo now finds, should he contact anything having to do with the surface world, that he will sneeze uncontrollably."

And then my master began to sneeze as well.

# EIGHTEEN

*And what is the professional wizard's greatest reward for completing a particularly arduous and dangerous task? Is it the accolades of a grateful populace? Is it huge amounts of gold and silver tossed about his feet? Is it the complimentary vacation in the pleasure gardens of Vushta, or his official removal from the tax rolls? Although all these other factors are important for the wizard to feel truly honored, they pale before the professional wizard's basic and oh-so-necessary demand: The stipulation that he never has to repeat that particularly arduous and dangerous task, or one even remotely like it, for as long as he shall live.*

*Truly professional wizards, after all, must set priorities.*

> —*from* How to Hire a Wizard and Still Profit from the Upcoming Netherhells Crisis, *by Ebenezum, Greatest Wizard in the Western Kingdoms*
> *(book still in progress)*

Someone knocked on the door of my sleeping room. Groggily, I asked who it was.

Norei opened the door.

"You have slept the clock around!" she called. "Get up! We will have dinner shortly!"

Dinner? How long had I slept? I pushed myself to a sitting position as Norei left the room. Now that she mentioned it, I was rather hungry.

It all seemed like a bit of a blur now. Once I realized that Norei had managed to alert Ebenezum and Hubert the dragon of the danger from the Netherhells, and the

two combined to send the fiends back where they had
come from, what energy I had left seemed to vanish
completely.

Oh, I had not gone to sleep immediately. I managed
to stay awake long enough to wash most of the slime
from my body and to watch them retrieve Vushta and
put it back where it belonged. But watching the city of
forbidden delights being set back into place had completely done me in. I didn't even remember making it to
my bed. I remembered nothing, indeed, before Norei's
knock.

My clothes were laid out on a chair. Apparently,
someone had cleaned them while I slept. I had to admit,
as I slipped them on, they felt much more comfortable
than they had for quite some time, but I found I missed
the torn bits of hat I used to keep within my shirt.

There was a scratching at the door as I moved about
my room. I pulled it ajar.

"Eep!"

"Eep eep!"

"Eep eep eep!"

The room was suddenly filled with adoring ferrets. I
laughed as they nuzzled my knees and ankles. I hoped
Norei would understand my need to keep these creatures
near me. Perhaps we could put them in pens so they
could still be close and not underfoot.

I walked from the room with a hundred ferrets at my
heels.

"Ah, there you are, Wuntvor!" Snorphosio called.
"Glad to see you're up and about. There's so many
things to organize, you know. Eventually, we'll even
have a dinner in everybody's honor, as soon as we can
get everybody together!"

I asked after my master.

"Oh," Snorphosio confided in a whisper, "he is in
the Great Hall, being cured by the greatest wizards in all
of Vushta."

I thanked the old wizard and walked down the cor-

ridor to the great oak door beyond which Ebenezum
was receiving his cure. I heard repeated, muffled sneezing. Apparently, they had not yet made it to the final
stage. It would probably be best if I did not bother my
master just yet.

I walked through the foyer and stepped outside.

"Oh, Wuntie!" Alea waved to me. She stood between
the dragon Hubert and one of the student wizards. I
walked over to meet them.

"Wuntie!" Alea repeated breathlessly. "Have you
met Tomm?"

I smiled in a vague sort of way before I remembered.
That was right! He was the one who gave up a life of
tinking! Well, I supposed he was a decent enough chap
with which to pass the time of day. We exchanged
pleasantries.

"Wuntie," Alea breathed, impulsively grabbing the
tinker's hand, "Tomm and I are going to be married!"

I could not believe my ears! The beautiful Alea was
going to marry this lout? For a moment, I was taken
aback. I wondered what she could see in someone as big
and stolid as that. What had the two of them done,
while I had been risking my life in the Netherhells?

"Yes," Tomm beamed. "My mother is very happy."

I mumbled my congratulations.

"But we have even better news!" Hubert added. "We
realize now that our original efforts describing your
journey may have been a little downbeat. So we've
brightened up the song considerably and made it a real
hum-along tune!"

The dragon blew an enormous smoke ring. He looked
as if he could no longer contain his excitement. "I suppose we could give him a little sample. Hit it, damsel!"

Alea once again sang in her clear, high soprano:

Wuntvor the apprentice, he's our kind of guy!
Awkward as he was, he still somehow survived!

I thanked them quickly, before they could get any farther, and told them I would rather wait and hear the entire song cycle at once, so that I might get the proper effect. To my great relief, they agreed and then began to tell me of the festivities in some detail. It seemed that, after one final discussion with my master, Klothus had decided to become a weaver. As soon as he finished three more robes in a certain silver moon-and-star design, Hubert assured me, he would straightaway begin a series of ceremonial costumes for damsel, dragon, and the guests of honor who would make the festivities grander still.

I began to think that, on the night of my honorary dinner in the Great Hall, I might find something to eat in Vushta.

I hailed Snarks and Hendrek, who had just stepped from the college.

"A beautiful day," the vast warrior said, looking aloft. "Doom."

"So everything's back to normal," Snarks added. "And as dull as ever!"

A great commotion came from a clump of trees beyond the college. "I found one!" a mild yet strong voice cried. "A wild pig at last!"

"Like I said," Snarks continued, "just like normal. I see they've got your master stuck in the big room over there. Is it going to do him any good?"

I assured the truth-telling demon that these were the greatest mages in all of Vushta. True, Ebenezum's malady was a little different from their everyday problems, but they would surely find a cure!

I walked below a nearby window that led to the Great Hall, anxious to hear these great wizards weaving their curative spells. Oddly enough, there seemed to be even more sneezing than before.

"Doom," Hendrek said. "So what do we do now?"

I assured Hendrek that, once my master was cured, he

would quickly be able to remove the curse from Headbasher. Snarks, it appeared, had been offered a post at
the extension school as resident expert on the Netherhells.

And then I thought, what would I do? Eventually, I
imagined, go back to the Western Kingdoms with my
master, study, and become a full-fledged wizard. But all
of that could wait a day or two. I was but a few minutes'
walk away from Vushta, city of a thousand forbidden
delights. Even though I had walked the Vushtan streets,
it had been at a time of crisis, and I had had no time for
sightseeing, much less going down one of those side
streets where a single errant glance might doom a man
for all eternity.

But I could correct all that now. It appeared that
Snorphosio was in charge of arranging the dinner in our
honor. If that was the case, I had all the time in the
world. And the time to see Vushta was now!

"Anyone interested in an afternoon stroll?" I asked
the others.

"Wuntvor!" a woman's voice called to me before
either of my compatriots had a chance to answer. Norei
walked rapidly across the lawn to meet us.

"I saw you out here with the dragon and that—
damsel." There seemed to be an edge to her voice.

I quickly told Norei about Alea's happy announce-
ment.

"Really?" The news seemed to cheer her considerably. "Still, I feel a bit sorry for the tinker. But that is
none of my affair. Wuntvor, may I speak to you for a
moment?"

We excused ourselves from the others.

"Wuntvor," Norei said softly as she gazed deep
within my eyes. "Do you have any plans for this afternoon?"

I mentioned that I had thought about going to
Vushta.

"Vushta?" Her lower lip trembled ever so slightly.

"But this might be the last afternoon we can spend together for a long time. Who knows what will happen after they cure your master?" Her fingers, somehow, had managed to intertwine with my own.

"Oh," I said. What was Vushta when I had my beloved by my side?

Then again, I remarked, perhaps I didn't want to go to Vushta after all.

Suddenly, there came a bout of sneezing so great that the outer walls of the Great Hall shook, as if not only my master but every single wizard in the room with him had sneezed at once.

"Then again," I added, "we may be here for quite some time."

We walked hand in hand toward the privacy of the trees.

"Wuntvor," Norei said sweetly. "I only have one question. Isn't there some place you could put these ferrets? At least for a little while?"